I0713104

COSCOM
ENTERTAINMENT

ALSO BY A.P. FUCHS

Undead World Trilogy

Blood of the Dead

THE AXIOM-MAN*™ *SAGA
(listed in reading order)

*Axiom-man
Episode No. 0: First Night Out
Doorway of Darkness
Episode No. 1: The Dead Land
City of Ruin
Of Magic and Men (comic book)*

OTHER FICTION

*A Stranger Dead
A Red Dark Night
April (writing as Peter Fox)
Magic Man (deluxe chapbook)
The Way of the Fog (The Ark of Light Vol. 1)
Devil's Playground (written with Keith Gouveia)
On Hell's Wings (written with Keith Gouveia)*

ANTHOLOGIES (as editor)

*Dead Science
Elements of the Fantastic
Vicious Verses and Reanimated Rhymes: Zany Zombie
Poetry for the Undead Head*

NON-FICTION

Book Marketing for the
Financially-challenged Author
POETRY

The Hand I've Been Dealt
Haunted Melodies and Other Dark Poems
Still About A Girl

COSCOM ENTERTAINMENT

WINNIPEG

ISBN 978-1-926712-19-2

PUBLISHED BY COSCOM ENTERTAINMENT
www.coscomentertainment.com
Text set in Garamond; Printed and bound in the USA
COVER ART BY MATT TRUIANO
INTERIOR "HAND" ILLUSTRATIONS BY A.P. FUCHS

This is for those who get their face kicked in for a living,
those who aspire to get a fist to the face while dishing it
out to the other guy, and to those of us
who like watching them.

AUTHOR'S NOTE

The following is a book about zombies, fighting and . . . well, that's about it. Although a story has been crafted to book end the tale, its main focus is blood, guts, UFC-style fisticuffs, monsters and cage matches. I mean, robots versus zombies is cool no matter how you lay it down.

Why did I write a book that's all about throwing fists? The short answer: I'm a guy and this is what we do.

Putting it a bit longer: I love kung fu movies, action flicks and, growing up, was a big time Jean Claude Van Damme fan, whose movies were a bit of both. *Lionheart? Bloodsport? Death Warrant?* Couldn't tell you how many times I watched those flicks. What I especially liked about his movies was they always had two things in common: he always learned to do the splits at some point during the film, and he always finished off the bad guy with that big 360°-kick of his.

I got goosebumps every time I saw that stuff. Nothing but adrenaline-charged fighting.

Even when I found out the other week they made a third *Universal Soldier* movie I was geeking out.

There's a magic to fight movies that you don't get anywhere else even with, say, superhero flicks. At the same time, they do have that *hero* quality, the one where the good guy lands the finishing blow and you geek out inside because the bad guy got what was coming to him.

Bruce Lee, Jackie Chan, Chuck Norris, Jet Li, Sly Stallone—they all equal fight magic. Battles. Primal violence that deep down we all enjoy—especially guys, the whole hunter-gatherer thing.

Action.

And that's what this book is about. It's an action flick told in novel form. It's a B-horror/martial arts movie blend stuffed between two covers.

Guys and fighting. Good times.

So with that said—

Let's get it on!

- A.P. Fuchs
Winnipeg
March 2010

BATTLES

ZOMBIE FIGHT NIGHT

BATTLES OF THE DEAD

1
THE PROBLEM

2037 A.D.

Mick Chelsey couldn't believe it had come to this.

He stood outside Blood Bay Arena, hands shaking. His left cheekbone hurt from when his wife, Anna, slapped him. She was right. He was pathetic, an addict and a downright lousy husband.

Some provider I turned out to be, eight hundred and twenty-one thousand dollars. I've gotten us in way over our heads.

The enormous stone structure of the arena loomed over him like a judge pointing a finger, condemning him to a sentence he wasn't sure he could face.

Eight hundred and twenty-one thousand dollars. How could any man repay that?

How could any man *lose* that?

For a moment he wished it was ten years ago and he could get back to being in his late twenties where the biggest bet he lost was a couple hundred bucks. But it was also ten years ago the world changed.

The story was different depending on who you heard it from, but there was a common thread that united them all: a Middle East chemical spill and a small town. Some folks said the spill occurred near some old tombs outside the town, the mysterious substance having washed over the rocks, drops of it leaking through the cracks and reanimating whatever remains there were within. The only problem Mick had with that story was if indeed this happened, how could these fragments of bone and dust suddenly get up and walk around and, better yet, move the heavy rocks away from the tomb entrance so the once-dead person could roam about?

Another tale said the spill occurred *in* the town as the trucker hauling the stuff was passing through. After the accident, the bizarre liquid running everywhere, all who touched it were transformed into something neither living nor dead, but caught somewhere in the middle.

Mick believed the latter story. There really weren't any other tales floating around out there that adequately explained it. Nothing plausible, anyway.

The undead had quickly covered the Middle East, all having a strange need to feed on human flesh. Those they didn't devour were changed—*infected*—and became one of them. Somehow, one got on a boat undetected. The infection spread. Soon nearly every country in the world was being overtaken by the mindless creatures.

The past ten years could have pretty much been divided in two: five years of conquest; five years of revival.

Nearly every superpower that had the capability wanted to nuke the creatures. This idea was quickly vetoed at a UN hearing because, given the instability of each nation and the frame of mind of the desperate leaders in charge, nuclear winter would have been sure to follow and humanity would have vanished forever.

Instead, the slow-but-steady approach was taken and troops were re-trained using Intel gathered from around the globe as to where the dead roamed, how they operated and how they could be disabled.

Working together, humanity unleashed its forces and slowly but surely overcame the creatures. Millions of troops went out. Less than a quarter of that came home.

Some of the undead were captured and kept for observation. Some were tortured for fun. Many were bought at a high price by Mr. Tony Sterpanko, a self-made billionaire entrepreneur before what the media had dubbed the "Zompocalypse" and one of the few who found a way to hang onto their cash when money became obsolete for a time. It was these few who led the world economically once order was reestablished, but Sterpanko was the leader of them all.

He began a little program for all who were willing to come and watch as humanity had its revenge on the undead up close and personal.

It was called Zombie Fight Night.

And the whole world was watching either at Blood Bay Arena or on TV or the Internet.

Fighters from around the world came to exact revenge on the monsters that stole their loved ones and ravaged their cities. Other creatures who once posed a threat to mankind now allied with it to destroy the remainder of the dead. Others thought to be fable now existed and came forward to battle, the Space-Time Continuum having gone bust thanks to the unnatural rebirth of that which was dead. Worlds and universes collided—or so the theorists said—and those out of folklore wandered into our world. Zombie Fight Night was the most profitable business on the planet.

Mick had wanted a piece of it. He had had a few bucks on his person during the whole time the zombies were in charge. On a whim, he took it to one of the earliest zombie fights. He won and doubled his money. He bet again, double or nothing, and won. He bet, he won. He bet, he won. For weeks he'd go to the fights, betting on all, winning most. Any losses were quickly recovered.

Soon he and his wife had so much money they could start a new life anywhere. Over four hundred grand.

Then double or nothing came a'callin'.

Mick had lost and couldn't pay.
Sterpanko wanted his head.

2
THE CURE

Two weeks ago:

Mick's head torqued to the side as a giant mitt of a hand came crashing across his face. His left eye nearly swollen shut and barely able to see, he spat out a glob of blood then slurped the rest into his mouth for fear of losing more. The skin around his wrists stung against the coarse ropes binding him to an old wooden chair.

"You pay or die," the seven-foot Native man in front of him said then brought another giant hand across Mick's face, this time on the jaw. Mick heard and felt a *crunch* inside as his jaw temporarily dislocated then slipped back into place. No blood this time. Just eyeballs that felt like someone was squeezing them from inside his head, and a brain that was no doubt on its way to swelling double its size if the beatings didn't stop.

The big guy stomped on Mick's foot, breaking his toe. Mick howled, but was quickly silenced as a twisted black rag looped over his head, found its way into his mouth, then yanked him backward tight against the chair. The chalky fabric was strangely soothing to the wounds within.

The behemoth in front of him stepped to the side and another man stepped forward from the shadows.

Tony Sterpanko.

"Good day, Mick," Sterpanko said, rubbing his palms together then bringing them across his head to smooth back his pepper-gray hair. He wore a dark suit, black button-down done up to the top, no tie. The man didn't look as old as he was. Mick could only imagine the cost of the Botox and dermatological care.

The mild crow's-feet on either side of Sterpanko's eyes suggested he once was a happy fellow. Though this was no doubt true—the guy bled green and had a dozen giant homes abroad; a new girl every night despite being married, and a business empire that spanned the globe—there was something else now in his gaze that made it appear those other things weren't enough or that something he held dear had been stolen from him during the Zompocalypse.

"I said, 'Good day, Mick.'" Sterpanko licked his lips then stepped to the side.

The big Native man punched Mick in the face, caught the chair on its way back, and brought Mick forward again. "You answer when the boss speaks, okay?"

Nose gushing blood, Mick nodded.

Sterpanko stepped forward. "Let's try this again: Good day, Mick."

Mick's head lolled to the side. *Answer him.* "Mrrmmm drrrgg." *Good day.*

"Close enough." Sterpanko bent at the waist before him, as if talking to a child. "You owe me quite a bit of money, Mr. Chelsey. Eight hundred and twenty-one thousand dollars to be exact. The value of such a sum is much more than it used to be." He smirked. "*Deflation,* you know."

"Irrrmm srrreee . . ."

"What was that?"

"Irrrmm srrreee."

"You're sorry?"

"Mmhmm."

"Well, then, I forgive you."

What? The pain swimming inside Mick's head

suddenly lessened.

"Actually, I don't," Sterpanko said. "If it was, say, eight dollars and twenty-one cents, I'd be happy to let you slide. Even for perhaps eighty dollars, but eight hundred thousand is quite a lot more than that. Even at eight hundred dollars I'd personally break your knees and wrists. Get what I'm saying?"

Mick nodded. *He's going to kill me.*

"Jumbo," Sterpanko said to the big man in the room. To Mick: "See, I do have a sense of humor." To Jumbo: "Mr. Chelsey owes me more money than most people see in their lifetimes. As you know, it is my business to calculate the cost of a life. Mr. Chelsey's is not worth nearly what he owes." Sterpanko's eyes brightened. "But if both him and his wife paid, then that should take care of the debt."

"Nhhmmm. NHHMMM!" Mick screamed against the gag. A hard swat to the face silenced him.

"No?" Sterpanko said.

Mick shook his head, tears leaking out his eyes.

"Tell me why not."

Anna. Not Anna. She's my wife. I love her. I made a mistake. No. Not Anna. Never Anna. No. No. NO! "Mrrrmmmgg . . ."

Sterpanko nodded to Jumbo. The gag was removed.

Mouth dry, the insides of his cheeks stinging, the taste of stale blood on his tongue, Mick could barely speak. "P-pl-ease. I beg you . . . d-don't." He licked his lips. "Not . . . wife." A whisper: "Kill me. Not her."

Sterpanko glanced up and pressed his lips together. He sighed. "You're fortunate I know what it's like to lose a loved one. You're *unfortunate* because I'm going to kill you anyway."

Like lightning, Sterpanko jerked his hips and a split

second later an Armani shoe caught Mick in the temple. The chair fell to the side, Mick along with it. His head hit the cold cement floor.

Darkness crawled over his field of vision and an intelligible whisper caught his ear as if Sterpanko was a hundred yards away rather than staring down at him.

The coppery stench of blood filled Mick's nostrils, keeping him in the moment. Coughing, he tried to get up, but wrestled against the ropes and the chair. *Still on the floor.* The puddle of blood oozing around his face was also running into his mouth. He envisioned the side of his head, the one against the floor, cracked open, blood and gunk slowly leaking out.

"Help me," he whispered. He didn't have the strength to say more. Just then what felt like two iron clamps had him by the shoulders. Vertigo set in once the chair was upright. The room spun; his vision was blurry.

A man stood before him. He looked familiar, but he couldn't place him. Then he recognized the voice.

"One night," Sterpanko said.

"One?" Mick whispered.

"It works like this: you get yourself together. We watch. You come to Blood Bay Arena. You start small. You try and win what you owe me. What you bet is what you get. If you get it all back, we're done. If you don't— even if you're off by *one* penny—I will kill you, your wife, and every single family member that might be wandering what's left of this planet."

Mick's heart ached. What Sterpanko was saying would be impossible. A continuous winning streak? Or winning nearly all the fights? He'd have to bet big. Huge. Colossal. Insane amounts just for the sake of this. He'd have to burn as bright as a candle's flame just before extinguishing.

He couldn't risk it. "Can you just kill me now?"

"I can, but I've decided to not spare your wife after all. Mine wasn't spared. Why should yours be? And your family? We'll find them."

You're sick.

Mick didn't have a choice.

Why was Sterpanko doing this?

3
READY TO RUMBLE

BLOOD BAY ARENA wasn't the kind of place you'd want to spend too much time around. From the outside, it was reminiscent of a Roman coliseum, round in shape, tall columns by the doors and windows. The difference was the concrete dome on top—a safety precaution, it was sometimes called—and glowing red letters mounted across the front entrance reading its name. The parking lot was packed nearly every fight night.

It was a place Mick knew all too well and one he didn't care to hang around anymore.

If he got out of this thing alive, that was.

Nervous as all get out, he made his way to the front doors, withdrew the ticket Sterpanko had given him from his coat pocket, and went in.

At first, Mick had wondered why Sterpanko even let him place his bets *at* the arena. For all intents and purposes, the tycoon could have held him and he could have just bet from whatever holding cell Sterpanko chose. But the answer became clear when Sterpanko informed him that, "Being a man of my word—and believing in old-fashioned luck—you'll conduct your business as usual." He cleared his throat. "I'm fully aware gamblers have their own habits and ticks, setting being one of the things that affects their instincts." With a smile: "I'm a sportsman and I'm going to give you a fair shot."

Well, fair shot or not, Mick was thankful he didn't have to spend any more time near the man. He wasn't a fool, though, and knew full well he was being watched to ensure he did indeed show up tonight and, more importantly, didn't skip town and immediately bring the death sentence on him and his wife and all those he cared about.

Passing through the main gates, Mick went shoulder-to-shoulder with everyone else, each person he brushed against or passed making him wonder if they saw the look of dread on his face.

Skin warm, a fine film of sweat formed on his back, a thicker film under his arms. He grabbed a program from a stand near a garbage can then checked his ticket. Section B, Row 9, Seat 2. Glancing up, he followed the letters on the hanging signs outside each set of doors that led into the arena proper.

"B . . . B . . . B . . ." he said. There it was. B. He went in and followed the short set of cement stairs down to Row 9. His chair was the second one in and so far only one other person was in his row. He glanced at his watch. 6:42 P.M. The first fight wasn't scheduled to start until 7:30. He knew gamblers. Anyone else betting in his row was probably just out in the hallway, calling their "banks" and ensuring their finances were in order before finally making their way in.

Mick sat down, opened the program and flipped through it.

Frankly, there wasn't really a strategy for these fights. The undead were unpredictable. It was easiest and more of a safe bet to roll with the non-zombie as the winner. Comparatively speaking, they did win most of the time. However, the zombies—even the Shamblers—weren't completely stupid and were known to come out on top now and then as well.

"Well, we'll see what happens," Mick said to himself. His thoughts wandered to Anna. The last thing she said to him was that she hated him. *She didn't mean it.* He knew that much. It was just anger. Her eyes were glazed over when she said it and her voice cracked. She was more concerned for their lives than for the money or even for what he had done that screwed them over.

"I'm sorry," he whispered, and pulled her picture out of his wallet. She was so beautiful. His finger traced the photo. The long brown hair set in loose ringlets, smooth skin, almond-shaped eyes—even that small scar on the side of her chin that she got from the Zombie War somehow accented her beauty.

Clenching his teeth, he closed his wallet and shoved it in his back pocket.

Mick glanced around the arena. It was starting to fill up.

It was getting close to showtime.

Up until now, Mick had been feeling more or less okay, but as his watch ticked off closer and closer to 7:30, the more it was as if the cockroaches in his stomach knew the first fight was about to begin and the more agitated they became. The feelings of regret and sorrow were quickly being shuffled away, replaced by pure adrenaline-charged apprehension.

This was it.

This was serious.

This was life or death.

Mick checked his watch: 7:27.

His heart raced into his throat and boomed against the back of his neck like no one's business. He could barely swallow never mind breathe and was forced to lean forward, elbows on his knees, head between his legs.

"Hey, buddy," the chubby guy beside him said. "Watch my shoes if you're gonna puke." A pause. "You know, the show's not even started yet. Unless you're getting flashbacks."

Mick glanced up at him, doing everything he could to control his breathing. "No puking here. I'm an old hand at this."

The chubby guy furrowed his brow, creating a nest of wrinkles. "Then why the huzzah?"

"Why don't you mind your own business?"

The guy put his hands up as if in surrender. "Hey, don't go looking at me for help if you lose yer guts tonight. Just wanted to see if you're okay, maybe."

Mick sat up in his chair and exhaled slowly. "No, you're right. I'm sorry. Been a long weird day, couple of weeks, to tell the truth. My bad."

The dude folded his hands over his large stomach. He smelled like hot dogs and spicy burritos. An invisible thick coat of smoke hovered over the guy's jacket as if from a lifetime of cigarettes. Mick stirred in his seat. The guy shoved a thick hand over to him. "Name's Jack."

Mick took the guy's greasy hand in his. "Mick." Firm shake, single pump. He took his hand back, making a conscious effort not to wipe his palm across the front of his shirt.

Mick pulled his Controller out of a pouch in the back of the seat in front of him and double checked the details of the first fight. The Controller was his lifeline tonight. It was a black box, about six inches square, with a screen and keypad. He swiped his I.D. card through a slot in the side. The screen lit up and welcomed him to Zombie Fight Night. It then displayed the list of fighters for the first battle.

Make it count, Mick thought, though for this first

match it wasn't easy to say who would come out on top.

He entered his bet and his choice of winner.

Please, God.

7:29. The seats in the place were full. The shoes and boots on everyone's feet—except Mick's—began thumping rhythmically against the cement.

Jack threw a couple of chubby digits into his mouth and let out a whistle.

The lights went out.

4
VAMPIRE vs ZOMBIE
BET: $5,000
OWING: $821,000

His name was Ramus, one of the few surviving "Others" ever since mankind regained control of their planet. Before the dead rose and conquered most of the globe, his kind had come first. The problem was, their type of infection—the vampiric virus transferred through blood—had to be administered blood-to-blood. Their victims had to be bleeding, which was no trouble, but the vampires had to be bleeding, too, which made things more difficult. It wasn't always easy to cut your own tongue before biting down on the neck of another. Instinct to just drink usually took over at that stage of the game and the act of biting down on one's tongue was often forgotten, which was unfortunate because if more vampires were made, perhaps fighting for the humans would be a thing of the past.

As it was with the Zombie War, mankind had quickly overcome the vampires by stakes through the heart. They had manufactured firearms capable of expelling steel projectiles a foot long at ferocious speeds. Soon, the number of known vampires worldwide was dwindled down to only a few pockets here and there. Eventually, they were captured and used for Zombie Fight Night as combatants. In exchange for performing, they were given fresh blood from murderers, rapists and thieves as a thank you for their participation.

It was dark in the arena, as it was before all fights. Ramus stood there, leather-clad hands clenched into tight fists, ready for the lights to shine and for his prey to rise into the cage. He took a step to the side, heavy boots scraping along the cement floor, his tight, leather one-piece suit squeaking a little as he did. He didn't care about the sound. Stealth wasn't an issue when facing off against the undead.

As much as he enjoyed the kill, he didn't care for administering death to something that was already dead. And the taste . . . well, he could stomach a lump of decaying flesh if it meant the sweet red nectar of human blood shortly after.

Overhead, the buzzer blared. The place erupted into cheers, clapping hands and hoots and hollers. The bright white lights flashed on, their focus on the cage. The audience was a mere shadow just beyond.

It was all automated as no human referee would dare enter the cage before a fight went underway.

The low whirring of mechanical gears filled Ramus's hyper-sensitive ears and his keen sense of touch picked up the mild vibrations in the cage's cement floor.

About fifteen feet away an iron ring four feet wide lit up bright blue on the ground. The ring slid to the side within the cement, revealing a dark hole.

The crowd hushed.

Growls.

Ramus knew what was about to come through.

Mechanical gears got to work.

The dead began to rise.

It was a Sprinter. Ramus could tell by the ghoul's pasty white face and bloodshot eyes and red irises. The other kind, the slower ones, were gray-skinned with deep shadows hugging their eye sockets.

The Sprinter immediately growled and roared and jerked at the electronic restraints shackling his wrists and ankles, the cuffs bound together with a short chain.

Any moment now someone off to the side would press a button and—

The buzzer went off again.

The shackles released from the dead man's wrists and ankles. They clanged onto the floor by the zombie's feet.

It was on.

The audience cheered, their stomping feet thundering throughout the arena.

The Sprinter charged toward him. Ramus waited until the ghoul was almost upon him before leaping over the creature's head and landing on the other side.

As it was with all fights, Mr. Sterpanko's words echoed in his head. *Give 'em a show, if you want your blood. Nothing quick.*

"Sprinters are never quick kills," Ramus muttered, spinning on his heels and backhanding the zombie across the skull.

The creature lurched forward, regained its footing, then whirled around and ran at him, arms outstretched, long dead fingernails zipping through the air like razorblades.

Ramus stepped to the side, kicked the creature in the back, then brought his heels together, sliding in before administering a side kick to the rear of the creature's neck. Bone crunched, causing the head to lean at an unnatural angle, but the ghoul didn't care. It turned around, growled, then ran around the perimeter of the cage.

"What's it doing?" Ramus said, remaining where he was.

The Sprinter darted in circles, at least a dozen times.

The crowd booed.

Give 'em a show.

Just as Ramus was about to make a run for the zombie, the Sprinter changed its course and came at him straight on, slamming its head against his. The force of the blow caused Ramus to bite down on his own tongue. Blood immediately filled his mouth. Something hard caught him in the jaw. A fist. Then fire lit up his midsection as the Sprinter tore its nails across his abdomen.

Ramus dropped to his knees and the Sprinter grabbed him under the jaw, jerking his head up and nearly separating it from his neck. A bone popped.

A toe broke as the Sprinter stepped on it. *Crunch!*

The Sprinter bit into his skull and tore out a chunk of flesh and bone.

Ramus licked his own blood from his lips and ignored the pain. "I don't think so." He'd heal soon enough anyway.

Quickly, he latched onto the zombie's shins, grabbed hard and pulled, tearing the dead man's legs out from under him. The Sprinter fell back with a thud.

Shakily, Ramus got to his feet and touched the top of his head. His fingers recoiled upon touching soft, squishy tissue.

Brain.

"You'll heal later," he told himself and then took off into the air. Feet together, he crashed down on the zombie's ribcage. Bone sliced through the dead man's skin like needles through a water balloon. Blood and fine strands of flesh burst upward.

The Sprinter's jaws snapped as it struggled beneath Ramus's weight.

Ramus tore off the glove on his right hand.

His shiny, black, talon-like nails glimmered in the overhead lights. With one powerful thrust, he dug them into the Sprinter's neck, ripping out the creature's trachea and holding the tubular windpipe up for the crowd to see. They cheered and whistled as the blackened blood dripped onto his face. He smiled, then stuck his hands in again, this time into the soft spot under the ghoul's chin. Hooking the nails in place, he ripped upward, tearing away the creature's lower jaw. Barely anything kept the creature's head attached to its body, its shriveled tongue hanging out like a severed worm.

Ramus pulled the rest of it away and brought the head to his lips.

Give 'em a show, Mr. Sterpanko said.

"Show's over."

Ramus bit down, dead flesh filling his mouth.

5
WHAT'S NEXT?

*C*RAP. "I'M A dead man," Mick whispered. *The Sprinter was supposed to have that one.*

"What?" Jack asked.

Mick sighed, his heart hammering inside his chest. "Nothing."

"You lost, didn't you?"

Mick nodded then cursed himself for doing so. *Revealing the outcome of your bet was against the rules.*

Jack slapped him on the shoulder. "Stay strong, my friend. The night's young." Jack glanced down at his Controller.

"How'd you do?" Mick asked, as if Jack's grin didn't tell it all to begin with.

"Little bit here, little bit there," he said.

Little bit. Hm. I don't have time for "a little bit." And he should keep his mouth shut. Five grand gone. Just like that. I'm down even more now. He bit his lower lip. *Money's not really an issue. Either I win and Sterpanko's happy, or I lose and can't pay him anyway 'cause I'll be dead. Got credit with the House. It's a game to Sterpanko. He'll let me bet all I want because either way he wins.*

Mick gripped his own Controller. "I'm in trouble," he said softly.

"Heh?" Jack said.

"Nothing."

"You say an awful lot of nothing for a guy who looks like he's got a lot of something on his mind."

Mick smirked. *Got to at least make my money back from the last fight.* "Double it," he said, louder than he meant to.

"Double it. You sure? Unless you're doubling ten bucks or something."

Try betting ten grand. "Or something." *Now keep quiet.*

Mick punched in his bet underneath the display of the upcoming two fighters.

He glanced around the arena. Some folks were still staring at their Controller screens. Others leaned forward as they slid them back into the pouch in the seat in front of the them. Yet others held their Controllers in their laps, looking elsewhere, as if holding onto them gave them a sense of control over the fight's outcome.

Ten grand, Mick thought. *Ten. Grand.* He rubbed his hands together. *Anna, if you could see me now.*

Actually, it was better she couldn't see him. She'd kill him before Sterpanko could if she knew how much he'd just thrown on the line.

Mick put his head between his legs and breathed in deep.

"Sure you okay, dude?" Jack said.

Mick didn't answer.

"I said—"

He abruptly sat up. "Yes, I'm fine, okay? Just back off."

Jack put his hands up. "Okay. Sheesh." Facing forward, "Guy tries to help you and you bite his head off. Yeah. Cool. Okay." He folded his arms and coughed while saying, "Fruitcake."

"What?"

"What?"

"What?"

"Yeah, I said, 'what'?"

"No, what did you just say?"

"Nothing."

"Nothing?"

"Nothing."

I know what you said. But I deserved it. "Sorry."

"It's cool, hombre. Just sit back and relax. You'll be fine. After this fight, beer's on me, 'kay?"

Might need more than just a beer if this next fight ends like the last. "Okay." Then, "Thanks."

Jack nodded. "Don't mention it." Softly: "You just owe me a ride home."

"What?"

"I didn't say anything."

The crowd switched from chit-chat to hollering. Feet stomped on the floor.

The lights went out.

6
SAMURAI VS ZOMBIE
BET: $10,000
OWING: $826,000

AKASHI YASUTOMO GRIPPED the handle of the *wakizashi*—his curved sword, shorter than his *katana*—with his right hand, the sheath with the other. Once the lights went on, it was time to reclaim his honor, something he had been trying to do for the last eight years.

A long line of honorable Samurai had come before him and though much of the tradition had been lost over the centuries, the Yasutomo family had been careful to maintain its integrity throughout the ages. Akashi had thought the tradition alone would have saved his family from the zombie hordes, but he was mistaken. Skill with the blade only took you so far. Sometimes there were things you couldn't fight and a legion of mindless, flesh-hungry drones was one of them.

The dead came one night when he and his family were sleeping. The children were eaten first, his son and daughter. His father's screams from the next room jolted him out of bed. Though a trained Samurai himself, his father was no match for them, not for the nine that invaded the room and attacked the eighty-one-year-old man who had lost the use of his legs thanks to an accident while battling another swordsman. By the time Akashi got there, it was too late.

The dead then came after him and his wife, and as he pulled her along to his room for his sword, they got hold of her. He kept running, grabbed his blade, hoping he'd have enough time to save her. Instead, he was greeted to the sight of her body hanging limp in a dead man's arms, half her face missing. Swallowing his emotion, he took the blade to them as best he could, but more and more came into the house until all his strength had been sapped and he had no choice but to flee.

Years of practice, years of training, all tested at once, all used for the first time that terrible night.

That was eight years ago and he had used his skills ever since, at first in Japan, defending those under attack by the dead when he could. Someone from Sterpanko's circle had seen him fight and offered him the chance to regain his family's honor in front of the world.

Though he was to remain humble and avoid the spotlight at all costs, he chose to consciously ignore those looking on at his battles and instead envisioned his family being his only audience.

He needed to do them proud. Do things right, the way he should have the first time.

The lights were still off in the arena.

The buzzer blared.

The crowd howled.

The lights went on.

Akashi tuned them out, canceling their roars until there was only him, the cage and whatever was about to come through the floor.

The iron ring lit up, slid to the side and the dead began to rise.

Gray-skinned with shadowy, sunken eyes and brown and black ragged clothes, the creature stood shackled before him. The thing just stared at him, gaze vacant, as if it didn't know what it was looking at.

I've done this long enough to know what you are, Akashi thought. *A "Shambler," they call you. No challenge. No honor.* He had heard a Sprinter was in the cage the fight before his. Now *that* would have been a battle worth fighting. Not this.

The buzzer droned again and the ghoul's restraints were released.

Akashi unsheathed his sword and got ready, bringing up his arms and sliding one of his feet back to a basic fighting stance.

The ghoul looked at its hands as if trying to register where the restraints had gone.

"I will not attack you," Akashi said. "You must attack me."

The dead man looked up at him. Hunger and a hidden rage suddenly filled the monster's eyes.

"Ah, now you see me." Akashi clamped his mouth shut. *No more talking.*

It was time to fight.

The zombie shambled toward him, steps awkward, arms outstretched. Akashi remained motionless, sword at the ready, waiting. The dead man drew closer, fingers splayed out, ready to grab hold of him and get to work devouring every chunk of flesh it could.

Groaning, the zombie lurched forward, arms coming down. Akashi ducked to the left, pivoted on his right heel, getting in behind the dead man. *Swish!* The blade came down, clipping off the zombie's ear. The crowd roared.

"Though I believe one blow is sufficient for victory, to simply end you won't restore honor to my family," he said. *That was for my daughter.*

The zombie put a decaying hand to its ear and didn't seem fazed by the gooey red-black blood sticking to its palm. It turned around, dropped its hands, then stomped toward Akashi like a gorilla.

Akashi stepped to the side, drew up his sword and brought it down on the monster's arm just as it reached out for him. The blade tore through muscle and bone, the arm landing on the concrete with a wet thud, blood quickly puddling around it.

The Shambler arched backward, growled, then set its dead eyes forward, fixated on Akashi.

That was for my son, Akashi thought.

The zombie ran toward him. Akashi brought the blade down. The creature caught his wrist with its remaining hand and shoved his arm and blade backward, the sheer force jerking at Akashi's shoulder socket. With a kick to the creature's gut, Akashi gained a few feet of distance and was able to yank his arm free. He put the sword in his other hand and let the other arm rest.

Quickly, he took a spinning stride forward, crouched, and swept the blade across the zombie's knees, cleaving the creature at both shins. *Thump, thump.* The dead man dropped, the bottoms of its legs missing.

For my father.

The zombie fell forward, arm out, and took hold of Akashi's ankles. Growling, it opened its mouth wide and moved to take a chomp out of his ankle.

Swish!

In a blur of silver, the blade swept *through* the zombie's neck.

The crowd went silent.

Thunk. The dead man's head dropped on top of Akashi's foot. He kicked it aside.

For my wife. Four blows. One victory.
Honor.

7
NACHOS

"Now that's what I'm talking about," Mick said. *Finally. Things seem to be going my way.*

"Did well?" Jack said.

"Well enough to—" He caught himself this time. *Or keep breathing, anyway.*

"Good for you."

Mick smiled.

"Hungry?" Jack said amidst a rush of voices from the crowd.

"What?"

"I said, are you hungry?"

"Oh, kind of, but not sure for what. You know, one of those moods where you want something, but anything you think of sucks?"

"I hear you."

"What do you normally have at these things?"

Jack snorted, sucking back what sounded like a full nasal cavity of snot. His cheeks puffed out and Mick could only imagine he had a loogie on his tongue. A moment later, Jack swallowed. Mick grimaced. Jack's eyes watered over and he shook his face as if he suddenly got the chills. He cleared his throat. "Um . . . no real usual. Pretty much tried everything on the menu. The nachos ain't too bad. Real cheesy. Sometimes the guy making 'em goes scant on the chips, but overall they ain't bad."

Mick scanned the crowd to see if he could spot the on-foot concessions guy. There was a dude dressed in a white milkman-type suit a few aisles over. Mick stood up and put his fingers in his mouth and whistled. Took a few tries, but he finally got the guy's attention. "Hey, buddy! Yeah. Nachos. Here." The guy in white nodded.

He sat back down.

"Good call. You know, he probably would have come over here eventually," Jack said.

"Yeah, but I need something to fill me up. Got butterflies." He didn't mean to say that last part.

"What, you won last round, though, didn't you?"

No comment.

"Then what's the problem?"

Mick pressed his lips together, then softly said, "No problem." He took a deep breath then exhaled slowly. It was time to choose. He grabbed his Controller from the back of the chair in front of him and scrolled to see the info released about the next fight. "Hm."

"You're telling me," Jack said, eyes glued to his own Controller.

"What do you think?"

"You know the rules."

"Sorry." Mick again pressed his lips together. Blood Bay Arena rules were that you spoke to no one about your bet. They had eyes and ears everywhere. Get caught choosing because of someone else's choice, or because you have someone on the inside, or get input from someone because they've seen one or more fighters on the roster fight already—never mind a number of other things—and not only did you automatically lose your bet, you had to pay back double.

Sterpanko didn't tolerate cheaters.

Only guys up to their hair in debt with him, Mick thought absentmindedly.

The next fight could go any number of ways. Well, two, technically. Either someone won or they lost, but *how* they won or lost was up in the air and that was a factor in betting as well. You could opt for just a simple straight win-or-lose when choosing your fighter; you could also choose whether you thought they would cream the other guy; and you could also choose how long the fight would last—all for bonus money.

Mick decided that for now he'd stick with what was simple: someone wins, someone loses. How it came about was up to them.

I've taken enough chances as it is, he thought.

The nacho guy came by. Mick set down his Controller on his lap and handed the guy his card. The nacho guy swiped the card on his handheld machine and waited for the transaction to go through.

"Sorry, but it's declined," the guy said.

"I see," Mick said. *Guess Sterpanko doesn't want me to eat. No sense asking him to try it again.* He held out his hand for the card. "Never mind. Thanks." The guy handed it back to him then wandered up the aisle to someone else whistling at him.

"I could have spotted you a couple bucks, you know," Jack said.

Why Jack was offering to help him out, Mick didn't know, especially since the guy was a bit of a jerk earlier. "Thanks, anyway, but I'm all right."

"Well, just let me know, yeah?"

"Sure."

Mick's stomach rumbled. He shifted in his seat. He glanced at the Controller, thought for a moment, then placed his bet.

Foot stomps and clapping filled the arena as fans got ready for another round.

"Here we go," Jack said.

"Yeah, here we go," Mick replied.

The lights went out.

8

THAI FIGHTER vs ZOMBIE
BET: $25,000
OWING: $816,000

Tep Baharn closed his eyes and got ready. He'd done this a hundred times before, each time demanding a courage no normal human being had within himself. Years of training and discipline only took you so far. Some things, some opponents, took more than just courage. They took the conquest of fear. Especially now, here in the cage, about to take on a monster yet again.

But this was what he was—a fighter, born as one, destined to die as one, whether here in the cage or as an old man all bent up and worn out from years of exchanging blows with opponents from beyond the grave.

After the rise of the dead, then after they fell, there was nothing left. No one left. His family had died in the attacks. His friends were gone. He had nothing. Nothing but the skills that saw him through the zombie invasion: hands and feet, elbows and knees. Though revenge was part of why he fought for Mr. Sterpanko, the main reason was to quench the inner need to simply tear apart what he could with his bare hands, a need he discovered deep within himself when it was just him, open land and a million undead.

He opened his eyes. The arena was dark.

The buzzer screamed and the lights shot on.

The iron ring suddenly shone bright then slid to the side.

The dead began to rise.

The creature rose to the surface, gray skin dusty and flaking, dark rings beneath its eyes.

Tep had fought Shamblers before.

Piece of cake.

The buzzer droned, the crowd cheered, the dead man's restraints fell to the ground.

Tep raised his hands, fists loose but ready, elbows parallel to the floor, forearms set to block anything the dead man threw at him.

The Shamblers all moved the same: one foot slowly dragged in front of the other, the feet slapping down heel to toe, arms swaying side to side like a pendulum until the creature saw what it wanted then reached out for it.

The zombie brought its hands up, then quickly brought one down, trying to get a grip on Tep's shoulder. Tep let it grab him and allowed it to pull him closer.

Closer.

Closer.

The ghoul opened its mouth, about to take a chunk out of Tep's neck. In a flash, Tep shot his elbow outward, clocking the creature in the side of the jaw. The jaw bone snapped. Then he quickly tagged it with an upper cut, knocking the creature's head back. The zombie brought both its arms in in an effort to grab him. Tep shoved the arms away, reached out, grabbed the zombie by what little hair it had left, then plowed the dead man's face into his knee. A front kick with his left leg and Tep sent the zombie stumbling back against the cage.

Some in the crowd cheered. Others booed and hissed. He couldn't blame them. Shamblers were only a challenge when there was more than one of them.

Usually.

The zombie pushed itself off the cage wall and

chugged toward him like a train going up an incline, its head low like some comedic bull aiming for that elusive red cape.

Tep stood his ground and let the thing stumble closer and closer, a false sense of tension for the crowd's benefit. Just as it was about to grab him, he moved to the side then in behind the creature and booted it in the backside, sending it sprawling on the floor.

The crowd laughed. Some guy from somewhere close said, "Gimme a break!"

Tep didn't care. This was too much fun.

The dead man got to his feet, turned around and came at him again. The monster's jaw hung from its sockets limp and weak and no longer a threat. Tep charged the creature and shoved it into the cage wall and wailed on it with his hands and feet. Each turning kick to the zombie's midsection shattered its ribs; each hook to its face broke the thing's cheekbones all the more. Fist. Elbow. Knee. Foot. Fist. Elbow. Knee. Foot. Fist. Elbow. Knee. Foot. Over and over until there was nothing more than a sack of bloody skin filled with shattered bone pressed up against the cage wall.

The zombie still tried to bite him, but with no working facial muscles—the most movement it got was some kind of relaxed twitch in his face—he merely curled and contracted his lips.

Tep dropped the creature and let him sprawl out on the floor.

It was over.

Piece of cake.

9
GETTIN' READY TO ROCK AND ROLL

YES! MICK HAD to make a conscious effort to stay seated and keep his mouth shut. He reminded himself that indicating you won was also against the rules. Sure, you could cheer, boo or hiss during the fight, but the personal outcome of it had to be kept to yourself.

Jack must have caught him grinning. "Good for you."

"I didn't say anything."

"Of course you didn't." Jack smirked then stared at his Controller for a moment. Mick wondered how the big guy did.

Anna would be happy. Hope so, anyway, Mick thought. As good as all of this was, though, the night was far from over and there was lots coming up, some of the fights, no doubt, making the past few seem like child's play.

He stood up and stretched his legs. Jack did the same.

When the two sat down, Mick glanced around for the nachos guy again. What he wouldn't give for a bite and a drink. His stomach growled and already the inside of his mouth was getting a bit sticky. Guess Sterpanko wanted him to sweat.

Mick tapped his palms against his kneecaps. "So . . . how'd you get into coming here?"

"Me?" Jack said. "Ah, you know, wanted to see what it was all about. Found out I liked watching dead guys get their brains beaten in. Found out I liked making money. Even, weirdly, enjoyed the heart-sinking feeling when you lost it. Yeah, I know, weird, but whatever. Point is, I like the fights. Where else can you come and watch these—I don't even know what they're called anymore, these guys that fight them—fighters? Adventurers? Blood-hungry mascots? Psychopaths—whatever—you know? Where else can you come and watch bizarre characters duke it out against guys who once took over this planet?"

"Yeah."

"Nowhere, that's where. I have no idea how the guys we watch get involved and, frankly, I don't care. I'm here for the thrill. And I'm nice and safe here in my seat, too. Just sit and watch and no one—no one being me—gets hurt. All good. Place a few bets, win a few bucks, go home and keep to myself."

"Where do you live? I mean, what area?" Mick asked.

"The upside of down."

Mick looked at him, brow scrunched.

"My answer when folks ask me that. Sorry. Nothing personal. Just like my privacy."

"No worries."

Jack eyed him for a moment as if to cement his point.

For a second, Mick wondered if Jack was going to ask him where *he* lived. Jack didn't.

Mick grabbed his Controller and scrolled through the screens until he landed on the just-released details of the next fight. He hated that Blood Bay Arena—namely Sterpanko—only released the who-versus-who just minutes before the next bout. Obviously, it gave the skunk an edge. *He* knew who was fighting. He paid them, after all. The guy—if he wanted, and probably did—could have all kinds of bets running on each fight, the information he had on each fighter giving him a huge advantage over every other patron in Blood Bay Arena tonight and no one could call him on it. Zombie Fight Night wasn't regulated. It wasn't like the old days when these types of things were.

The very thought of it made Mick grimace. He hoped he pulled through this evening. Perhaps, if and when this was settled, he could somehow settle things with Sterpanko.

Personally.

He closed his eyes and suppressed the thought. No point getting all worked up over it right now. There was a fight to bet on and he didn't want to lose.

He wondered how Anna was doing and if she was still mad at him. He could envision her doing one of two things: either sitting at home, watching the fights on TV—despite how much she hated them—or frantically pacing their living room, wondering if he was going to come home alive. Either one would fit her character. Just all depended on her mood, and with her, when she was mad, assumed actions were hard to peg.

Mick studied his Controller and absorbed the details of the next fight. This one should be interesting. One of the fighters was an old hand at combat, and *old* was an understatement. The fighter might not be grandpa-old, but given his lifestyle, well, surely leading the life that he had would have aged him far more than your average person. It was a tough call. Each fighter had their own type of advantages. That's what made these fights frustrating to bet on: they were more or less evenly matched, but sometimes the show-boating went too far. The fighters got careless and more than money was lost.

Mick took a deep breath and soaked in what he read.

He placed his bet.

"Ready to rock and roll?" Jack said, leaning over to Mick as he finished replacing the Controller in the back of the seat in front of him.

"Ready like always." *Kind of.*

"Then this one should be good."

"Should be."
"Hope so."
"Yeah."
A couple of minutes later, the arena went dark.

10
AXIOM-MAN vs ZOMBIE
BET: $100,000
OWING: $791,000

IT HAD BEEN thirty-one years since it all began, his quest against evil and to stand up for those who couldn't stand up for themselves.

Thirty-one years. A long time to be doing what was right, to place oneself on the line day in and day out, by anyone's reckoning.

But that was what Axiom-man did. It was who he was. The call, the gift from the messenger to use his powers wisely—there was no other option, not even when the world fell apart and the dead rose to conquer the living.

Axiom-man had fought, battled, did everything he could to slow their advance and try and save as many lives as possible. It hadn't been the first time he had gone up against the undead, but he certainly hoped it would have been the last. Day in, day out. Night in, night out. Sleep—there were times when three or four days would go by before he got any and at his age, sleep was as precious a commodity as air.

He had to be extremely careful. All past encounters with the undead demonstrated that if they took a bite out of him and swallowed his flesh or blood, they inherited his powers. Not right away, but eventually. It was dangerous not just for him, but for all who sat under Blood Bay Arena's roof.

Even now, standing in the dark inside this dank arena, he felt the subtle tingle of fear encompass his heart. His costume no longer gave him the confidence he needed. Dark blue tights, light blue cape and mask—they used to be a symbol to a city that was crumbling around him. Now . . .

His body wasn't what it used to be, not with permanent nerve damage throughout one arm and leg on the right side of his body, and not with being blind in his left eye. Years of service, years of pain. Many of the scars were only skin deep whereas others were forever embedded within, contained in a heart never fully to be mended.

He should have saved the world. He could have. He had seen the zombie uprising play out on another world. He could have warned humanity. Could have made preparations, but he did none of that. There was no one on Earth more powerful than him. His strength, his gift of flight, the energy beams he could project forth from his eyes—all tools that should have served humanity as they made their final stand against armies of the undead.

Sure, humanity prevailed, but at what cost? Billions were dead. Axiom-man himself had saved tens of thousands of those. But everyone else? He should have saved them, too, or at least died trying.

He supposed that was why he did this now, fighting, beating up on the undead for sport. Still a chance to punish them for all they stole from not only himself, but from the whole world as well. It was just too bad these fights were not just battles of the undead, but also entertainment. He could use his strength, use his flight, and only use his eye beams to nick his opponent instead of blow them apart.

"Don't want to make it too easy for ya," Sterpanko had told him back when he started. The only reason Axiom-man listened was because Sterpanko knew his true identity after an ordeal involving him saving Sterpanko one evening while the dead walked the earth, the battle having torn up his costume so much that most of his face was showing. Well, a photoscan on a cell phone and a few computer searches later and Sterpanko knew it all. To keep the identity a secret, Axiom-man had to put on a good show. By now, keeping his identity a secret wasn't about protecting those he cared for. Nowadays, it was about protecting himself and the world over. He could only imagine a world that knew who he really was, the people who'd constantly beat down his door whether in an attempt to harness his powers somehow or merely use him to accomplish things they could do on their own. At first Sterpanko had wanted to use his knowledge of his secret identity to get him to fight, but had to switch to Plan B when Axiom-man had gone along with it voluntarily.

The buzzer went off.

The lights went on.

The crowd cheered, the older folks in their seats chanting Axiom-man's name, many with smiles on their faces. The younger crowd, they just wanted to see blood. They hadn't been around when being a symbol in a cape meant something.

The iron ring shone bright then slid to the side.

The dead began to rise.

It was a Sprinter.

Axiom-man hated these guys. Shamblers were no big deal unless there was more than one of them. Sprinters, however, well, they presented their own challenges, namely in the areas of speed and just plain all-out ferocity.

The buzzer sounded and the Sprinter's restraints fell to the floor, clanging against the cement.

Axiom-man almost powered up his eyes on instinct, but remembered the rule he was bound by: no eye beams.

Fine. He clenched his fists, locked his feet in place and got ready. An instant later the Sprinter shrieked and darted toward him, bloodshot eyes wide and unblinking, fixated on his own. Teeth bared, the creature lunged for him. Axiom-man stood his ground and shot out both fists, summoning all his strength. His knuckles barely felt the impact as his fists plowed through the Sprinter's chest, embedding themselves in the dry, rotting flesh and bone beneath.

Axiom-man yanked his arms free and flew over the dead man, landing on the other side.

The crowd went wild.

The Sprinter teetered to the side then spun around, swiping its hand in the process. The back of the zombie's hand caught Axiom-man across the chin, sending the world into a spin. He dropped down to one knee.

"This never used to be this hard," he muttered. His knees protested as he tried to stand, the arthritis nice and aggravated. He stood anyway.

The zombie pounced on top of him. Axiom-man got his arms around the creature in a bear hug, hoping to squeeze the thing hard enough to at least break more ribs. The problem was, judging by the severe decay all along the zombie's face and neck, this one had been dead for quite sometime and—*snap, snap, snap*—the ribs broke like kindling and didn't faze the creature.

The Sprinter opened its mouth wide and made a move for Axiom-man's neck. He'd been in this position with these things before and knew exactly what to do. He jerked his head to the side, the creature getting a clean

bite of air. Next, he shoved a palm beneath the zombie's chin, forcing its head away. Axiom-man wriggled beneath him and got his own face against the zombie's chest, his mouth hanging over one of the holes he had punched in it earlier. The inside of the monster stunk of rotten meat and foul fish.

Axiom-man held his breath and used his other hand to sock a new hole into the creature's body, this time into its kidneys. His fingers met dried flesh; he gripped hard and ripped his hand out, tearing with it what he assumed was the remainder of the kidney that once occupied the space.

"More! More! More! More!" the crowd chanted.

Grunting, Axiom-man floated off his back, taking the creature with him, and slammed it up against the roof of the cage. He flew out from underneath it and let the creature drop to the cement below. Swiftly, he darted back toward the ground, aiming to land on the back of the zombie's neck and use his heel to separate the creature's head from its body. Instead, the dead man rolled to the side and Axiom-man's boot firmly planted into the ground. Fiery pain raced through his foot and up his shin and into his knee. A loud *SNAP* echoed in his ears.

He collapsed, an inferno of pain wracking his right leg.

The Sprinter darted toward him, arms out, and latched onto his shoulders. It brought its head in. Axiom-man raised an arm to block it. The creature bit down onto his right hand and tore it free from his arm.

"Gggrraaaahhhh!" Axiom-man shrieked. Blood spurted from the wound in wild arcs, painting the cement red.

The place went into an uproar and he wasn't sure if it

was over the thrill of seeing blood or over what just happened to him.

Heart racing, body and mind already sinking into shock, the instinct to survive took over. Axiom-man powered up his eyes and readied himself to blast the creature.

The rule, he thought. *Screw the rule. I'm going to die! I'm going to—*He looked at what was left of his forearm. The creature—if it had ingested his blood, soon enough the thing would have his powers.

He couldn't let that happen.

He let the energy blast forth from his eyes, cauterizing his wound. The stench of burnt meat and fabric made him gag.

The zombie finished devouring the last of Axiom-man's hand.

Shaking, Axiom-man knew he couldn't stand so instead floated to his feet, right foot blazing with pain, right arm limp at his side.

"This could be the last one," he whispered. "The battle is finally over."

He flew as fast as he could toward the creature, leading with his left.

WHAM! They collided. The two went sailing through the air. The Sprinter slammed up against the hard wire mesh of the cage.

Axiom-man kept pushing and forced the zombie through it like garlic through a press.

11

SO, WHAT DO YOU DO?

*Y*ES! MICK WANTED to jump up and kiss someone. But he didn't. Keeping his best poker face, he closed his eyes, pictured Anna, and thanked God for the help.

He thought he heard a low rumble in Jack's throat, but couldn't be sure.

"Washed up, bugger," Jack muttered.

Washed up or not, Axiom-man had this one, Mick thought. But he was also bitten. Will he turn? Do zombie bites affect him? I could only imagine a world with a zombie Axiom-man, a zombie with superpowers. I hope it works out for him.

It was hard to discern by Jack's tone if he was happy or mad. Whatever the feeling, Jack didn't show it.

Jack rubbed his hands together quickly; the rough skin of going palm-on-palm was like sandpaper on a piece of wood with the bark still on.

"So what do you do for a living?" Mick asked.

Jack stopped rubbing his hands together, sat back, folded his arms and said, "What didn't I do?"

"Retired?"

"You kidding? Not now nor ever. Besides, we all had a taste of retirement when the dead ran things."

"Yeah, because running for your life and hiding out is so relaxing."

"But no work."

"Was work to me. Don't know about you, but running the hundred-meter dash in under ten seconds is work for anybody. 'Least it was for me."

"But you didn't punch a clock everyday."

"No. Just zombies."

Jack smirked. "Didn't we all."

"So seriously, what do you do, if you don't mind me asking?"

Jack smacked his lips. "Little of this, little of that. More of an odd-jobber now than anything. Used to be a lawyer back in the day."

"Really?" Mick scratched his nose.

"Aw yeah. A darn good one, too."

"Put anyone away?" Mick realized how stupid the question was after he'd said it.

"Naw, not me. Did more office stuff than anything. Contract law. I'd go to court, sure, but it was more about reaching settlements, staring down the other guy, that sort of thing. Boring, those days were. Long hours. Gained a ton of weight. Lost it during the Zombie War then got it back."

"I think we all dropped the pounds pretty good back then. No food. Lots of running. Body wanting to give out. Not healthy losing, either. The bad kind. The kind that kills people."

"If they weren't eaten first."

"Yeah, if they weren't eaten first."

Jack cleared his throat. "And you?"

"Job?"

Jack nodded.

"Before the war I used to paint cars. Was the guy in the white suit in the shop. All alone. Maybe had help once in a while. Small shop. Nothing fancy. But we did do custom jobs so it was a blast trying to take the client's design and make it work in 3-D. What folks who came in never realized was that some of that stuff only worked on paper. Cars move in different ways, their bodies. Not just linear—you know, flat—like paper. Had to take the contours and stuff into account before painting something special. Anyway, rambling. Point is, yeah, that's what I did. Was fun, too. Then the war came and the shop I worked in was blown to bits during one of the army's efforts to eradicate the undead. What'd you think happens when you blow up a place with loads of paint under pressure? Big explosion. Was not far from the shop when it happened either. Didn't actually see it, but I sure heard it. Huge boom. Then there was this big orangey-yellow glow against the sky followed by a whole crap ton of black smoke. Nasty." Mick swallowed, his throat dry. What he wouldn't give for something to drink. "After the war . . ." He didn't want to say it, but Jack's expression was that the guy was genuinely interested in what he had to say, so Mick rolled with it. "After the war I got into, um, coming here." With a smirk, "You're sitting in my office."

Jack chuckled. "You're sittin' in mine, too. Guess we're co-workers."

Mick chortled. "Guess so." He thought about prolonging the joke, but held his tongue when he noticed Jack's face go straight. The big guy leaned forward and grabbed his Controller. Mick did the same. Once he got to the appropriate screen, he wasn't sure if what he read about the next fight was correct, so he backtracked to the beginning and logged in again. When he got back to the details of the next fight, he was surprised that what he had read the first time was indeed accurate. He'd heard about this upcoming fighter but never saw him. There was a first time for everything.

How do you bet on something like this? "Man . . ." he said then shut his mouth, hoping nobody heard him.

Jack appeared lost in his own Controller screen.

Mick thought long and hard about who he was going to pick for the next bout. He also knew that whomever he chose, he was going to have to bet big to take a sizeable chunk out of what he owed Sterpanko. Immediately he got warm. Sweat oozed from his pores, making his clothes stick to his body. A shiver ran through him.

Just make the right choice, he thought. *Yeah, no kidding.* He thought about it once more then made his bet. *You better be right, man.*

Mick put the Controller away just as the lights went out.

He leaned back in his seat and gripped the armrests.

Feet stomped on the floor. Folks cheered.

It was time to begin.

12
MINOTAUR vs ZOMBIE
BET: $155,000
OWING: $691,000

The dark reminded him of the labyrinth from long ago, the one built for King Minos. He hated it. Thankfully, those days were long over.

One night in the labyrinth a strange shining blue portal appeared. The Mintoaur thought it might have been summoned by the gods, but he could never be sure. Out of curiosity, he entered the portal and emerged in a world overrun with humans, many which feasted on each other.

The Minotaur stood up proud in the dark, breathing heavily through its nostrils. The dark never bothered him. If anything, it was an ally, especially during battles in the night when men struggled to see. To the Minotaur, night was home.

Despite what people thought of him throughout the ages, he was *aware* and not just some mindless beast roaming here and there, destroying whom he chose, establishing punishment on a species that kept him in a maze for years and years and years. There was more to him than people thought. He only played the beast card because he could.

The zombie uprising was just punishment on mankind, he thought, and he enjoyed joining the dead in conquering the living. Over the years he also followed them to what he only referred to as their hive, but was soon rounded up by men with rods that, when they poked him with them, lit up his flesh in sharp pain.

Now, he was told, he was to fight these walking dead men and women or else the men would kill him.

Regardless of the threat, the chance to hunt a fearsome creature regularly appealed to the Minotaur on a primal level and it was something he was more than happy to indulge in.

Now, captured, he was forced to settle for becoming an enemy of those which he once helped, so instead devoted his life to destroying the dead shells of human beings when he was let out of his cage.

The buzzer droned.

The lights went on.

The crowd hooted and hollered when they saw him. His presence was always a special treat.

The iron ring shone then slid to the side.

The dead began to rise.

A pasty-faced female rose through the floor, her blonde hair wild, her eyes wide and bloodshot. There was no humanity left in her gaze.

The buzzer sounded again and the dead woman's restraints fell to the floor. So did the Minotaur's.

It was time to begin.

The Minotaur dipped his head and gusted out two sharp breaths through his nostrils. Digging his heels into the floor, he pushed off against the pavement with all his might and charged toward the Sprinter. Head bowed, horns cutting through the air, he came at her with all he had. The woman shrieked and ran toward him to meet him head on. The Minotaur ducked his head down even further. Faster. Faster.

Sploish!

His horns punctured deep into her chest. The woman's body jerked wildly as he straightened then arched his head back, thrashing her limp body about. *Thwoopt!* The Sprinter flew off his horns and crashed into the cage wall. Her body smacked the floor and blood quickly pooled beneath her.

The Minotaur approached her, knowing full well this wasn't the end. The woman lay there, face down, two large wet holes as big as saucers on her back. One was by the shoulder blade, the other lower and more toward the middle.

"Get up," the Minotaur said.

The Sprinter remained motionless a moment longer before slowly getting to its feet. The dead woman looked down at her chest and roamed a pair of white fingers around the bloody holes. Her mouth opened wide as if to scream, but all that came out were raspy gasps.

The Minotaur raised his large hand and slapped her across the face. With the other he sent an upper cut into her chin. She flew back into the cage. Grabbing the chain-link with both hands, she shook it, once more releasing a raspy gasp.

She released the chain-link and came at him. Sharp nails on bony fingers tore into the Minotaur's flesh, slashing his forearm to ribbons. Another white hand went for his chest. He moved to block it, but her hand and arm were so small and so quick she went around his parry and dug her nails into his chest, digging hard and deep into the left side. The woman ripped her hand out, taking with it a mash of skin, flesh and blood.

The Minotaur stumbled back and a collective "Ooooh" swept over the audience.

His heart rate quickened. He placed his hand over the hole in his chest. Any deeper and the woman would have ripped out his heart and part of the rib covering it.

It had to end now.

He lowered his head, gravity forcing blood to gush from the wound.

He charged.

Just as his horns were about to slice through her midsection, the woman leaped into the air and landed on his back, her weight sending him sprawling on the floor. Fist after fist beat upon his shoulder blades and the rear of his neck, tearing and ripping.

The Minotaur put his hands beside himself, disbelief and shock that a creature so small had gotten the better of him flooding his system, and pushed against the floor in a kind of push up.

A sharp pain tore into the back of his neck, hard and different.

Not nails from a bony hand.

Teeth.

13
THE OLD GUY BESIDE HIM

Mick WISHED HE had a gun. One bullet. Right to the temple. Oh, just to have it lodge in his head and end it. Nothing but blackness then a bold step into the afterlife.

As *manly* as he tried to be, the tears brimming the bottoms of his eyes brought him down about fifteen levels and back to the way he felt when he first got here tonight. Actually, he felt worse since he was now deeper in debt than when he first got going on the fights this evening. He turned his head so Jack wouldn't catch him on the edge of a breakdown.

A few moments later, Mick grabbed his Controller and verified that he did indeed lose the last fight.

How could a Minotaur lose to a freakin' zombie? That was like a dog losing to a squirrel. Even though the sucker was a Sprinter, a zombie was still a zombie, and muscle was still muscle. The Minotaur had had enough muscle to pulverize the dead woman no problem. Stupid mistake? Freak luck? Whatever you wanted to call it, that Sprinter took the big guy down and now Mick was paying for it.

He glanced at Jack. The guy was grinning ear-to-ear.

"Have a good time?" Mick asked.

"Can't say who I picked, but who would have known hitting the wrong button would . . . well, you know."

"Good times," Mick muttered. He could only imagine Jack's payout right now. No one in their right mind would have opted for the Sprinter last round. But David versus Goliath stuff still happened and the last fight decided to be one of those times.

"""

He was glad Anna wasn't with him. She'd tear out his throat for the way that one went down.

He wanted to call her, check in, and assure her he was still alive and still in the game.

If you want to still be in the game, you're going to need to really crank things up and bet with nothing to lose. He sat up straight and folded his hands between his legs. *Nothing to lose. Guess that's my new strategy now. Gonna have to pretend it's just me, no Anna, money's not owing and not give a rip about the outcome. Live. Die. Don't matter. All the same.*

Oddly, there was something liberating about the notion. Who would have thought apathy could be its own therapy?

"Gonna go to the john," Jack said. Then, with a wink, "Save my seat."

"No worries there," Mick said.

Jack left.

The guy on Mick's other side was a wrinkly geezer that looked about a thousand years old. If the guy's skin was any paler, the old-timer would pass off just fine as one of the dead. Huge, black visor-like sunglasses hid the man's eyes. A neat little tuft of white hair sat on the man's head like a dollop of whipped cream. The old coot kept his gaze fixed forward, cane between his legs, hands folded atop it. The man's dark red coat, as big and thick as a blanket, appeared cozy and warm.

Mick thought about introducing himself, then thought better of it. He didn't want to appear to whomever was watching him that he was having too good a time or was getting friendly with everyone around him.

He sat back in his seat and folded his arms. Without the smoky smell of Jack's jacket, the old guy beside him emanated a strong odor of ancient skin and warm meat.

The old guy kept staring forward. Part of Mick

wondered what he was thinking about; another part wondered if the guy was dead. The Controller directly in front of the man was lit up, so the guy was definitely betting on something. Maybe the old-timer was a Zen master or some such and was meditating.

Mick rubbed his hands together and pulled out the Controller for details on the next fight. He hated what he saw. It was one of those bouts that flipping a coin would give you the same chances as consciously choosing.

"One for the money, two for the show . . ." Mick said. *Three to get ready . . .*

He played out the next fight in his mind's eye as best he could. No one delivered the final blow. He'd have to wing this one.

Jack came back and plopped down beside him with a heavy sigh.

"All's well?" Mick said though he didn't know why.

"Didn't fall in."

Mick chuckled.

So did Jack. "How much time?"

Mick checked his watch then double-checked the time of the fight on the Controller. "Not much."

"Let's see here," Jack said and took his Controller from the seat in front of him.

Mick put his eyes back on his own screen. "And four to go," he mouthed.

To get out of the hole he was in, he'd have to bet gigantic.

Apathy is my policy. He laid down a ton. If he won, he'd be on his way to the top.

If he lost . . . he'd be on his way to six feet under.

The lights went out.

14
ZOMBIE vs ZOMBIE
BET: $300,000
OWING: $846,000

Even the dark was covered in a sheet of red. Bloody and inky.

The Sprinter didn't have a beating heart, but his pectoral muscles, like the others in his body, still seemed to work and they, in place of his heart, rapidly twitched their own twisted beat.

A low growl lingered in the back of its throat, one based on rage, fueled by an anger that had rooted itself in its rotting intestines since the day he was reborn.

One of his nostrils was plugged, the cartilage having rotted through a long time ago. When, he wasn't sure. Sometime during the . . . he didn't know the word for it and only had images: blood, the tearing of flesh, people running, screaming. But the other one worked, just differently than . . . than what he couldn't remember. The scent was on the air. He didn't need to breathe it in through his nose—he couldn't breathe—but the air made its way into his nostril and touched the olfactory nerve cells. What was left of them, anyway.

Decaying meat. Fat and sluggish.

The buzzer sounded and the lights went on.

Dark red to fire red.

Noise all around as countless voices cheered and hollered.

The iron ring lit up then slid to the side.

The dead began to rise.

A gray-skinned pusbag that must have weighed over four hundred pounds stood before him, its smell so sharp it was no wonder he smelled the creature before it even rose through the floor. The dead man across from him was greasy, with a balding head covered in sticky thin strands of unwashed hair. The guy's rolls hung over a pair of pale blue boxer shorts, the bottom of his gut nearly touching the knees of his stubby legs. Rotting man-boobs with dried-up nipples hung low and off to the side from his chest. The dead man had no neck, but instead his fat head, no longer appearing to be supported by neck muscles, sank into his shoulders.

Delicious.

Fattie raised his hands to just below his gut, the shackles restraining him jingling as he did.

The buzzer sounded and the shackles fell.

Lunch time.

Fattie just stood there, as if unsure what to do. All the Sprinter saw was a bag of powdery gray meat hanging off a rack of bones. If the Shambler had a beating heart, the Sprinter was sure he would hear it.

The Shambler stumbled forward, its steps lame and slow. Only a few inches at a time.

The Sprinter charged him, mouth open and teeth ready. He raised his hands out to the side and hooked his fingers like a set of talons. He plowed into the fat man, his teeth gouging the flesh of the man's chest, his fingers digging themselves into the man's sides. The Sprinter tore out a bite. Black blood oozed from the corners of his mouth.

Cheering resounded.

Fattie dropped his head and smacked him in the forehead. Bone cracked and the Sprinter wasn't sure whose skull gave way. Perhaps both. He withdrew his fingers from Fattie's sides and checked his forehead. The skull was dented with a sharp ridge down the middle, but it wasn't split wide open.

A heavy set of thick slabs for arms closed in swiftly from the sides and locked him in from the elbows up. The Sprinter jerked and squirmed and, as fast as he could, pulled his arms out then shot them in, digging his fingers into the fat man's sides. The moment his hands were in the cool flesh, he grabbed hold of whatever he could find then tore them out in a splash of black blood. The liquefying remains of a kidney, liver and some intestine splattered to the floor.

The Shambler groaned and dropped its head again, this time pushing a set of teeth into the top of the Sprinter's shoulder. Flesh tore then was removed.

The Sprinter took the pain, fought once more against the Shambler's hold, and, still unable to break free, slammed his head up into Fattie's neck, taking as much into his mouth as he possibly could. The spongy texture of rotted flesh touched his tongue. Instant euphoria flooded through him.

The Sprinter chewed, swallowed, then pushed his face further into the blubber beneath the fat man's chin and slowly ate his way into the man's neck. The head was detaching. Just when he thought he was about to eat through clear to the other side, gravity took them and four hundred pounds of dead flesh pulled him down with it. They hit the cement floor with a resounding smack. The Sprinter felt the front of his skull give way upon impact. Then something else.

Something heavy fell from his skull as if his head was taking a dump.

It was his brain.

15
THE BALD GUY IN THE SPIDER-MAN SHIRT

Mick WANTED TO take a baseball bat to his head and bash his own brains in. How could he have been so stupid? Was it the Controller? Did he mistype?

Zombie versus zombie, a ridiculous fight that should never have happened to begin with. And now he lost, owing over three hundred grand more than the original debt that landed him here at Blood Bay Arena in the first place.

Careful to not show any emotion, he checked the Controller and verified his input for the last bout. As if Sterpanko would buy the excuse of a wrong-betting entry anyway. Mick had meant to choose the Shambler over the Sprinter. The idea was the Shambler's baser instincts and tolerance for pain would allow it to plow through any of the Sprinter's assaults and just go to town on the other zombie's neck. Subconsciously, though, he opted for the Sprinter and that ended up being his bet. On some level there was comfort. He *knew* better despite his mistake. Perhaps he could get that instinct to work for him as the night went on.

He glanced over at Jack. The man's brow was furrowed, deep creases on his forehead. Mick took in the old guy on his left. No expression. He just sat there, staring forward, hands on his cane; the epitome of tranquility. Maybe he *was* dead?

A part of Mick expected that any minute now one of Sterpanko's cronies would come along, scoop him out of his chair, take him to a backroom somewhere and beat his brains in.

No. Sterpanko's probably enjoying this, Mick thought. *He knows exactly how I'm doing. Probably torn between being ticked over my losing and being overjoyed that he'll personally put a bullet between my eyes. After he carves me like a turkey, that is.*

Mick stood up. "Excuse me, Jack."

Jack pulled in his legs and Mick ebbed out onto the aisle and made his way up the concrete steps leading to a pair of doors at the top. He went through them and went a ways down the wide hallway beyond to the bathroom. There was a line trailing out the door, but nothing too terrible. He could wait. More than anything he just wanted to splash some cold water on his face. He hoped that wouldn't be too telling to the other patrons.

As he stood there, hands in his pockets, Mick once again caught himself eyeing everyone else, wondering who, if anyone, was in the hole deep like him. The men in line, the other men and women walking by—they all looked as if they had it together.

But it's all surface. Remember that, Mick thought.

He followed the line into the bathroom, did his thing, washed up, then came back out. As he followed the numbers hanging above each doorway leading back into the arena proper, he ended up bumping into the guy in front of him, a burly guy, over six feet with a gargoyle tattoo on his neck.

"Sorry," Mick said.

The guy gave him a sour look and Mick thought the dude was about to deliver a giant fist into his kisser, but instead the guy stepped to the side and let him pass. Once ten or so steps away, Mick glanced back over his shoulder at him. The guy was already caught up in another conversation. A white guy with no hair and sunglasses wearing a Spider-Man shirt stepped passed the man Mick bumped into. Mick recognized him as he had been in the john with him.

Mick kept going, stopped for a sip at a water fountain, then looked back in the direction he came. The Spider-Man shirt guy stood not far off, looking at posters of fighters on the wall next to one of the entrances back into the arena.

"Uh huh . . ." Mick said, clucked his tongue, then picked up his pace.

He silently counted to ten then peeked over his shoulder again. The Spider-Man guy was not far behind him, walking.

"Great," Mick said. *Sterpanko's sent someone to come and do me in early.* "Fighting's not even over yet." *Guess he thinks it's hopeless. Coming to collect now, it seems.*

Heart leaping into overdrive, Mick made a conscious effort not to look over his shoulder. Quickly, he weaved in and out of the crowd, zig-zagging his way toward the entrance to his section, hoping he'd lose the guy.

Carefully, he feigned needing to check a sign on the wall thus enabling him to glance out his left peripheral to see if the guy was still following him. The bald guy was not far off, appearing as if he was searching the crowd, looking for something particular.

"Couple more gates," Mick said quietly. He hoped he could lose him. Then again, if the guy really had been sent by Sterpanko then he surely already knew where Mick's seat was.

He pictured the Spider-Man guy following him to his seat, causing some trouble and Jack coming to his rescue. Then he thought about how lame that was and if the guy behind him was indeed a leg-breaker of some kind, the guy was obviously a professional and Mick was in for a world of hurt if he was caught.

Mick darted between a few more people then dipped down and slipped off into the entrance of his section. He didn't look back to see if the Spider-Man guy was behind him.

He reached the end of his aisle. "Ex—" The words caught in his throat. "Excuse me."

Jack tucked his legs in.

Mick went to his seat, but not before noticing the Spider-Man guy coming down the steps toward his section.

Just stay calm. Just stay calm. He exhaled through pursed lips and eased himself onto his seat, expecting any second now to be asked to "come with me, please" and taken to some backroom and beaten worse than he had been before.

The Spider-Man guy was a few steps away.

Here we go, Mick thought.

The Spider-Man guy was at his row.

Mick pretended not to see him.

The man went past and went to a seat a few rows ahead of Mick's. The guy sat down and began talking to another man beside him.

"Hot out there?" Jack asked.

"Hm? What?" Mick said.

"I said, is it hot out there?"

Mick tried to catch his breath. "Um, no."

"Did you run?"

"What?"

Jack pointed toward Mick's forehead. Mick put his fingers to his skin. It was soaked with sweat. "Oh, ah, no. Just . . . yeah, hot, but not out there. Lots of bodies in here. Fight coming up." He quickly busied himself with his Controller. There probably wasn't long before the next bout and he had yet to place his bet.

"Tell me about it. I probably lost fifteen pounds just sitting here." He tapped his round tummy with his palms. "Not that I'm complaining."

"Why not take your jacket off?"

"Um . . . it's a thing I do. The jacket. Can't say too much else, right?"

"Right." Mick smirked then flipped through the screens for info on the next fight. He whispered, "This one's easy."

"What's that?"

"Nothing."

The lights went out.

16
BRUCE LEE vs ZOMBIE
BET: $127,000
OWING: $1,146,000

UIET AWARENESS. THAT would be the secret, especially now, standing in the dark, waiting for the opponent to unveil itself.

Bruce Lee grimaced and got himself ready, fists clenched but not tight, arms strong but loose, like iron chains with iron balls attached to them.

He'd seen these creatures before. He was almost one of them when he first arrived here. He remembered the night at Betty Ting's house, working. He had a headache so she gave him a painkiller called Equagesic then lay down. The blackness of sleep was suddenly invaded by a bright blue flash and then he found himself on the street, the buildings and cars unusual, smooth, fast. People ran around, screaming as others with white or gray skin chased them down. These "other" people were easy to escape and fight, so easy that after learning what happened and what they really were, he opted to further enhance his skill by fighting them regularly. He only hoped that one day he would find a way home.

The air danced across his naked chest. He mentally checked his feet; they were planted yet light, and he could move at a moment's notice if he had to. His knees were slightly bent beneath his black pants.

The buzzer sounded and the lights went on.

The iron ring lit up.

And the dead began to rise.

This one was different than the others Bruce had seen. It had the deep gray bags under its eyes like the Shamblers, but had pasty white skin like the Sprinters. A hybrid? Did they crossbreed? *Could* they crossbreed or did someone else *make* them?

I have no fear of opponent in front of me, he thought then transferred that thought throughout his entire being. *I have made up my mind and you'd better kill me before—*

The buzzer sounded and the creature's restraints clanged to the ground.

Bruce brought his hands up, on guard, and calmly eyed his opponent. He had to be ready for anything. He knew the Sprinters' and the Shamblers' ways inside and out since he'd been studying them. But this one . . . this one was different. Whomever made it—if they hadn't made themselves—might have even made it just for him. Every other one of the dead's number he had obliterated in under a minute, the Shamblers often in under ten seconds.

The creature took a step toward him. Immediately Bruce slid his foot along the floor, keeping his weight balanced, body guarded, ready for anything. Side-stepping in a circle, Bruce evaded the first lunge from the creature. The thing growled as it missed and quickly swatted a meaty hand toward him. Bruce slapped it down and instinctively his foot flashed out, connecting squarely under the zombie's chin from the side. The thing's head snapped back, the rear of its skull lulling over the back of its shoulder blades for a moment before slowly righting itself.

The crowd roared.

Bruce moved in to make quick work of the creature with a swift back fist to its head. He struck the thing's temple, knocking the head to the side. The zombie's arms lashed out. One hand swatted him in the shoulder, sending him briefly off balance. The other caught him by the neck. Bruce grabbed its wrist with one hand, snapped another back fist to under the thing's arm with the other, then quickly took advantage of the creature's momentary looseness and did a straight arm bar where the zombie's shoulder met its torso, twisted and folded its arm and shoved the creature to the floor.

Before the zombie landed backward with a wet thud, Bruce was already in the air. The moment the back of the dead man's skull cracked when it hit the cement, Bruce landed on its ribcage and with a loud, jaguar-like growl, squished the zombie's lungs.

The audience went silent.

It appeared the fight was over much quicker than everyone had anticipated.

Bruce eyed them all.

A small vibration in his foot let him know all was not what it seemed. The zombie grabbed his ankle with one hand and pressed against his knee with the other, sending him tumbling back. He hit the concrete hard. About to flip his legs under him to get up, he was swiftly knocked down again by the zombie, who shouldn't have been able to get to its feet so quickly.

The monster got on top of him and dropped its weight over him. Just before the creature's head descended to meet his own, Bruce got a forearm against the thing's neck. He pushed against the creature's weight with all he had. Snapping jaws surged forth then retreated in front of his eyes, every push against the creature getting harder and harder.

Bruce let go with everything he had and sent a sharp left hook across the creature's head. Black blood splooshed out of its mouth. The force was enough to allow him to pull his other arm away from the creature's neck. He came back with a right hook, stopping the still-traveling head going one way and sending it back the other.

A double punch to the chest forced the creature to re-shift its weight, allowing him some breathing room underneath it. Like lightning, he came across the zombie's head again, this time knocking the thing off him.

Bruce flipped onto his feet, kicked the creature in the head then raised his leg to stomp it into oblivion. Just as his foot sped down, the zombie opened its mouth. Bruce quickly adjusted and allowed his foot to stomp hard right beside the creature's head. He brought his other foot to the other side and squeezed the skull between his feet.

With an animalistic cry and a quick twist of the hips, he broke the zombie's vertebrae and the momentum was enough to tear the decaying flesh around its neck, severing the head from the body.

The cage stunk of blood.

Bruce spat on the creature as the crowd cheered.

Gung fu is gung fu, he thought. *It's not child's play.*

17

THE OLD MAN JUST SITS THERE

ENTER THE DRAGON, Mick thought. "Man, that was good."

Jack nodded. "Ayuh."

It was probably a safe assumption that Jack won as well. When Bruce fought, it was a no-brainer. Even the very few times the spry Chinese guy was challenged, he quickly was able to pull through. Bruce was the man. Pure and simple.

Mick checked the old man next to him for any sign of emotion. The old timer was as still as a lead weight, eyes still hidden beneath those giant dark sunglasses, head faced forward, hands still on his cane.

Is he a prop placed here to throw me off? Mick wondered. He nudged Jack, and whispered, "What's this guy's story?" He thumbed over to the old man.

Jack took a gander. "Don't know. Seen him around here. Sits wherever like most of us. Never talked to him. Never heard a name. From what I hear, he never speaks. Could be a mute."

"Friendly?"

"Don't know."

"Nothing?"

"Nothing."

"Hm." Mick stared at the old man. The guy hadn't moved. "He's not dead, is he?"

Jack let out a loud chuckle. "No. I think I might have seen him scratch his nose earlier. Could have been my imagination, too, though."

"Haven't even seen him reach for his Controller."

"Me neither, but that doesn't mean he hasn't. Part of being here, right? You don't just come to watch. That's for the folks at home."

"Yeah."

"How old do you think he is?"

Mick let his eyes follow the deep creases in the old man's face. You could stick a coin in there and it'd hold. "Probably dead-hundred and ten."

Jack chuckled again. "Maybe Santa's gone anorexic and he's sitting here. That hair is white, man. White-white."

"Like snow." Mick leaned back to the center of his seat. He didn't know why the old man bothered him so much, though that *non-movement* was definitely a big part of it. The guy could be a mannequin in a department store no problem. Put straw on him and stick him in a garden and your crops would be one hundred percent safe.

Mick leaned over a couple inches toward the old guy. Out of the corner of his eye he caught Jack watching him. Mick took a deep breath. To himself: "Okay." To the old guy: "Hi, how are you?"

The old man didn't reply.

"Name's Mick." He held out his hand.

The old guy nodded.

Movement. Good. He's alive. He let his hand linger in the air a couple moments before taking it back. "Having a good time?"

The old guy nodded.

"Can I get you anything?"

The man shook his head slightly.

"Okay, well, you just let me know. I'll be right over here."

The man didn't respond.

"I said, you just let me know, 'kay? I'm right here."

The man didn't nod.

Probably part deaf. "Okay, then." He went back to Jack. "Well . . . he's alive."

"Yup."

"Doesn't talk."

"Nope."

A pause. "Wanna say something?"

"Nah. Besides, he's too far."

"Too far?"

"Have to shout over you."

Mick put his hands up and wiggled his fingers. "Ooooh. Oh no."

Jack grinned. "You about done? We got another fight coming up."

"Yeah, well, at least I said something."

Jack grabbed his Controller.

Mick did the same. "All right, who's up next?" He flipped through the screens. "You got to be kidding me." This was a new one for him. He hated having to consider new fighters. Especially this one. Zombies were unpredictable despite what popular media had taught leading up to the Zombie War. Even Shamblers weren't as dumb as most people made them out to be. They weren't geniuses, but their instincts were sharp, so sharp you'd almost think it was some kind of intellect. As for the Sprinters—their smarts were different. Still instinct, but driven by rage and an obsessive need to exercise that rage. It *had* to be expressed. Sometimes, even after a kill, even after tearing up a body, it'd sit or scramble amongst the leftovers, slapping them, ripping the pieces even smaller, biting the blood-soaked ground, as if trying to kill the person all over again.

This next battle was a tough one. It didn't matter

though. He was still in the hole deep and he was about halfway through the evening. It was time to pick up a big shovel and dig himself out of the pit. It was either that or he'd soon find himself in yet another hole, that one six-feet deep.

If there was something left of him to bury, that was.

Mick took another second to think about it then placed his bet. A big one. The biggest one so far. If he won, he'd be well on his way to celebrating. If he lost . . . suicide was a serious option.

He put the Controller in the pouch in front of him then sat back in his chair and folded his hands across his stomach.

The old man beside him still gazed forward.

Jack coughed.

The lights went out.

Initiating scan.

Activating infrared sensors.

Scan complete.

Body heat: Negative.

Object: Humanoid.

Cross-referencing files.

Reading: Dead life form.

External sound: monotonous tone.

Metal on concrete.

Activate combat program.

Engage.

The R-1 stood there, seven feet tall, the combined weight of its parts tipping the scales at over four hundred pounds. It raised its mechanical arm, only now noticing its bright silver metallic body was covered with the flesh of freshly-dead corpses and then sprayed with blood for good measure.

Its objective: annihilate the dead.

Fresh from the factory, this was the R-1's first fight.

The robot raised its right leg and stomped down a large, heavy metal foot toward its prey. Then the other.

Advance.

Each footfall thumped against the concrete. At first it appeared the zombie in front of it—a deceased headbanger in a torn black Metallica T-shirt—didn't know what to make of the machine, its sunken dead eyes inside deep purple sockets conveying a sense of puzzlement.

The robot advanced again, and suddenly the zombie became alive with hunger, opening its jaw impossibly large as if it had been broken just prior to its death and rebirth.

Quickly, the zombie plodded forward on unsteady legs and lashed out its arms, grabbing hold of the robot by its motor-powered wrists. Immediately, its yellow teeth mashed down on the metal. *Crunch.* When the dead man removed its mouth, teeth like popcorn kernels spilled out the corners of its mouth.

The robot pulled its arm away with a quick servo-jerk then brought in its opposite arm and clamped its lobster claw-like left hand around the zombie's neck.

Bzzt.

The claw snapped closed, cutting the dead man's head from its body.

The moment the zombie's head thunked against the floor, boos and hisses filled its audio receptors.

The cacophony of a displeased crowd remained on the air for precisely 38.3 seconds before an echoey voice spoke over the intercom system.

"Ladies and gentlemen, welcome to Zombie Fight Night."

The crowd booed even louder.

R-1 refocused its audio receptors to separate the audience's disappointed shouts to zero in on the voice coming from the speakers above the cage.

"We here at ZFN are ready to rock your world with a fight like nothing you have ever seen before!"

The moaning crowd lowered their volume a little.

"That was just a sample. Tonight, and tonight only, we bring you not one, not two, not three, not even four—but five *fights in one! Five fights! Five battles to the finish. Five undead bodies take*

on the R-1. Five! Please place your new bets now or don't do anything if you wish to let your original bet ride."

Just then the iron ring in the cement lit up and rolled to the side.

A new zombie emerged. Its shackles sparked, the jolt enough to cause it to step to the side.

The ring descended then returned with another zombie. Another spark and this one, too, bounced to the side.

Three more times the ring disappeared, each time reappearing and bringing with it another of the dead.

There were three male, two female. All hungry. Two of the men were Sprinters, while the remaining three were Shamblers.

"Ladies and gentlemen, it begins!"

The buzzer sounded.

The shackles on all five of the dead clanged to the floor.

The R-1 analyzed its prey, sorting each by perceived threat level.

Priority: Sprinter x 2

Maneuver: ?

It wasn't programmed to take on more than one of the undead at a time.

Recall.

Priority: Sprinter x 2

Maneuver: ?

The zombies marched toward it.

Recall.

Priority: Sprinter x 2

Maneuver: ?

One of the male zombies, a Sprinter, locked onto its leg, chomping down on it like it was a soup bone. R-1 raised its leg with the zombie still attached and hyper extended its steel-coated fingers of its right hand until sharp blades popped out. It dug the blades into the Sprinter's back and pulled out a chunk of flesh. The Sprinter stopped biting for a moment then went right back to it. This time R-1 shoved its blades into the back of the creature's skull, squeezed, and tore out its brain.

The Sprinter stopped moving.

R-1 kicked the body off its leg and into the air where it collided with a Shambler coming toward it.

A female Shambler slapped her hands on R-1's shoulders from behind and began climbing up its back like a ladder. R-1 reached back and stuck its bladed hand into the creature like a fork and jerked her over its shoulder. It slammed the body on the ground. Just as the Shambler was about to get up, it stomped on its head, sending out a spray of bone and brain matter into the feet and ankles of the other female Shambler stumbling toward it.

R-1 brought forth its pincers and activated the servo-mechanism on its wrist. A soft whirring sound accompanied the now-spinning claw, turning it into a bizarre kind of drill. R-1 stuck its spinning hand into the female Shambler's face, stirring up the bone and flesh like decayed stew in a mixing bowl, the hand splooshing out the back side of its skull until its force was enough to spin the head right off the neck. A stream of black blood shot up from the neck and the body dropped to the floor.

The male Sprinter was off to the side, digging its fingernails into the chest cavity of the last Shambler.

R-1 advanced toward it with heavy, mechanical footfalls. When the Sprinter caught sight of it, he picked up the Shambler's body and threw it at the robot. The Shambler glommed onto the R-1 like an octopus around its prey, the creature still very much alive in undeath . . .

and hungry. It brought its heavy head down where a coating of flesh was wrapped around R-1's neck. It bit through the meat, its powerful jaws enough to crack the metal casing around the robot's neck and into the wires beneath.

Bright blue sparks shot up and around the robot's face. Some struck the zombie's skin, burning it in the process. It didn't care, and kept on eating.

The Sprinter came in, jumped into the air, and struck R-1 feet-first in the chest, sending the robot crashing backward against the pavement. The Sprinter dove into the other side of its neck and began working its way through the metallic casing on that side.

Recall.

Priority: Sprinter x 2

Objective failed.

Maneuver: Rotating claw.

Target: Head. Nearest dead life form.

R-1 drew up its still-rotating wrist and shoved it into the back of the Shambler's skull. Within seconds it stirred up the head and brain, leaving nothing but a mass of chewed up bone, stringy flesh and oodles of black blood. The Shambler's body stopped moving.

The rotating hand went for the Sprinter. The Sprinter swatted the mechanical arm away. R-1 went in again. The Sprinter pulled away from its neck, grabbed the rotating arm and tore the spinning pincers from it. Like a wild man, the Sprinter struck R-1 until its visual sensors blacked out. Only the left sensor came back on when the backup optical sensor kicked in. Disabled, R-1 activated the arm-blade; machete-like blades protruded from its arm from shoulder to wrist on its right side.

Internal sensor 1a: Power failing.

The Sprinter worked hard on R-1's neck, devouring

the flesh coating it as well as the wires beneath.

R-1 swooped its bladed-arm in from the side, connecting hard with the Sprinter, cleaving it nearly down the middle of the length of its body. Its skull split in two and toppled to the side like a sliced watermelon.

Objective: Complete.

19
BEING A KID AGAIN

MICK PUT A hand over his mouth in an effort to stifle his heavy breathing.

"That's so unfair," he said quietly. *What about those who just won on their original bet? Is there a payout? Hard to have "let it ride" otherwise. Sterpanko's cheating.*

"Shhh . . ." Jack said.

"What?"

"I heard you."

"Which part?" Had he said it aloud instead of thought it?

"What part?"

"Yeah, what part?"

"The unfair part."

Mick was relieved. "But it is."

"I know."

Mick bit his tongue and was convinced this was Sterpanko's move against *him* and the whole place was now paying for it.

Whatever. As if you expected this to be easy. Just roll with it. Okay, fine. So now we're getting somewhere. Won that last one. Good. Movement. Progress. Yeah, good stuff. Onward and upward and all that. Stop rambling. But if I had put down more . . . . No, can't think like that.

Amidst the booing during the last fight thanks to that surprise announcement, he *was* going to bet even more. But if he lost he'd be in way worse and recovery would have been nigh impossible so he kept his bet as was. During that last bout, though, he didn't know if the robot would make it. Machines were capable of so much, but that was the problem: *so much*. Once the limit was reached, that would be it. This was one of the reasons he had a hard time buying all those end-of-the-world movies—especially now since he'd gone through an apocalypse firsthand—you know, the ones with robots taking over the globe with mankind at their mercy. In the end, machines were still machines, each with limits, each with a power source. All someone had to do was pull the plug and one person usually did with those Electro-magnetic Pulse things. Why they never pulled the EMP out at the beginning of the movie and just won never made sense. But then there wouldn't have been a movie, now, right?

Mick's breathing slowed. He pulled his hand away from his mouth.

Jack sat slouched beside him, hands on his gut, twiddling his thumbs. The man merely sat there, staring ahead, subtly tapping his top and bottom teeth together.

Bad round, Mick thought, yet Jack also seemed the kind of guy who could keep a pretty mean poker face if he wanted to.

Mick glanced down at his shoes and, while tapping one foot, did a quick calculation as to where he was at with Sterpanko. *Not where I'd like to be.*

He wondered what would happen if he ended up winning big today and came out on top. Would Sterpanko pay him or would any extra won be moot? A part of him thought he might make a big stink about it if he ended up coming out ahead. Another part thought he'd just pretend he never got in the black and would hopefully go home with a blank slate. And even if he did win huge and could have pocketed, say, fifty grand or something, he couldn't tell Anna. She'd either be mad at him for not trying to keep it if he forfeited it—after all, every dollar counted as

they tried to re-set up their lives after the Zombie War—
or she'd scold him for taking it because that kind of
surplus would be too much of a temptation for him to
come back to Blood Bay Arena and blow it on more
fights. Mick hated to admit it, but Anna would be right
about that last part. He had the bug. He loved the thrill,
the "what if?" and the amazing gratification that came
from scoring big on a fight you thought you'd lose.

Jack cleared his throat. "You listening?"

"Huh?" Mick said.

"Seems they're changing things up a bit."

"What do you mean?"

"Last one had more than one zombie."

"Yeah. Maybe they're trying to make it more fair. I
don't remember seeing a robot take on more than one at
a time." *Fair. Yeah right.*

"Either that or that bucket of bolts had a few
upgrades so they had to compensate."

"That's what I just said."

"What?"

"About making it more fair."

Jack arced an eyebrow. "No, you didn't."

"Yes, I did."

"No, you didn't."

"Yes, I did."

"No, you—look, point is, things are changing up a
bit. Got it?"

"Don't give me lip, man."

"I'm not."

"Yes, you are."

"No, I'm not."

"Yes, you are."

Jack huffed and crossed his arms.

Mick grinned to himself. Tonight might be the last

night he could act like a kid. He figured he might as well.

He pulled out his Controller and checked to see what was going down for the next bout. When he found the screen, he took a long hard look at it. Some of these fighters—he couldn't help but wonder if they were set-ups of some kind, actors on Sterpanko's payroll. The Space-Time Continuum truly held no meaning anymore, at least not in the way it used to.

Regardless, here he was, in Blood Bay Arena, life as the world used to know it totally screwed up, puked out and messed up.

He thought about his bet. It'd be great if he could drop what he owed by at least half.

His fingers had a hard time committing to the Controller's buttons. Once a bet was placed, there was no do-overs, not even if you made an honest mistake and mistyped something. What was done was done. Game over, win, lose or draw.

Mick forced his fingers to comply with his thoughts.

He put the Controller back and waited for the lights to go out.

20
VIKING vs ZOMBIES
BET: $225,000
OWING: $569,000

Abel Meginbjörn stood strong, the weight of his chain mail shirt nothing he wasn't used to. Neither was he clenching the handle of his sword. At least, not yet. Not until the dead rose. He'd battled many times before, first against men of lesser standing, most not knowing how to wield a sword or axe to save their life. Stealing from them had been easy, whether it was precious metals, food, women or drink. But those days were behind him now. He didn't quite know what happened to his comrades. One moment they were sailing the sea, laughing, drinking and scouting the horizon for land. Some of his friends were known for ritually sharpening their blades before an attack, whereas others preferred their fists and hadn't used their knives and swords the last time they made landfall and took what they wanted. So there, on the sea, he gazed off into the darkening sky, sharpening his blade, the mist of black rain hitting the water somewhere off in the distance.

A bolt of lightning cracked overhead. Thunder followed. Then another bolt struck the ship, right where he was standing, striking his sword. A shock raged through him and all went bright blue, then white, then he was in a land not his own. Those he encountered on the ravaged streets suggested his armor would do him well as there were straggling "dead men" about. He encountered one, too, his shield protecting him from the ghoulish man's snapping jaws and sprays of blood coughed up from between cracked, yellow teeth.

The thrill of running that dead man through left him hungry for more, and as time went on, he discovered he was quite good at it and so eventually made his way here to fight the dead every chance he was allotted.

Abel Meginbjörn didn't care much for going home. Not anymore. Why pillage a small town or settlement when you could earn so much more by slaughtering the dead and protecting not just oneself, but the living as well?

He adjusted his helmet so it sat more comfortably on his head, enabling him to see just a little bit better. His helmet. Someone who was part of this . . . fighting circuit . . . showed him a picture of what was supposed to be a Viking. The fellow in the picture had horns sticking out of his helmet. Where such a notion came from, Abel didn't know. It didn't matter. He was here now, setting history straight, showcasing to those looking on that Vikings were not to be trifled with.

As he stood there in the dark, he wondered how many of the dead he would have to fight today. Sometimes there was just one, usually the slow ones, which he found to be an insult. One quick swipe with his sword, a splash of black blood, and the creature would drop. The other ones—Sprinters—were much worse, but still manageable thanks to his armor. Two times in the past he had to fight two of the dead, both Shamblers each time.

The buzzer sounded and the lights went on.

The iron ring lit up.

And the dead began to rise.

Two of them. One a Sprinter. The other the slower kind, it seemed.

"For my country, for my men. Today I will cut off your heads!" Abel shouted, raising his sword, gripping the handle tight. He ran toward the dead men.

The crowd shouted and cheered. "Kill! Kill! Kill! Kill!"

"GRRRAAAHHHH!" Abel growled and ran his blade through the shoulder of the slower, dead man. The other one, the Sprinter, was gone.

Abel whirled around, bringing his blade about in a wild arc. He connected with something and a moment later took note of the severed arm on the floor. The Sprinter in front of him shrieked and charged at him, fingers curled good and stiff, sharp nails ready to tear through his flesh, chain mail or not.

Abel moved to the side and the Sprinter moved past him, burying its hands into the chest of its slower counterpart. The Viking drew up his sword and ran it through the back of the Sprinter, piercing both that zombie and the one beyond.

The dead men twisted with the impact and black blood and globs of flesh splashed onto the floor.

Tugging at his sword, Abel hoped to rip it out then bring it up and around for a swipe at the men's heads. The blade wouldn't budge; the dead men's torsos twisted, one to the left, the other to the right, his sword lodged between flesh and bones.

Quickly, Abel brought up his shield and brought its heavy metal frame down onto the Sprinter's head, crushing its skull. The dead man beyond groaned and tried to pull itself free from the sword. Instead, it only tore up its torso, globs of lung, stomach and intestines splashing onto the concrete floor.

Abel withdrew his soax and plunged it into the slower man's head. The dead man's eyes went wide . . . then he went limp, his body still hanging on the sword.

"Boooooo . . ." the crowd droned.

Abel guided the dead men to the floor, placed a heavy foot on the Sprinter's torso, braced himself, then yanked hard, jerking the blood-covered blade out of both men's bodies.

"Boooooo . . ." the crowd continued. Others hissed. Many stomped their feet in protest.

Let them howl, Abel thought. *The world is now less two evils.*

The buzzer droned and instead of the cage opening as always, it remained shut.

"Boooooo . . ."

The lights went out.

A few sharp whistles from the crowd, then a few more. Soon the whole place began screaming, "Kill! Kill! Kill! Kill!"

Abel didn't know what to make of it. This wasn't how things went. He held his sword at the ready, his soax also gripped tightly with his other hand.

The iron ring lit up, casting blue light on a shadowy figure rising from the dark. This wasn't a zombie, or, at least, didn't seem like the others. This one was wider and wore something on its head.

The buzzer droned and the arena lights went on.

Primal cheers crashed through the air. It was all Abel could do to concentrate on what was before him.

A dead man.

A dead brother.

Another Viking, this one with the red eyes of a Sprinter, glaring at him from beneath a tarnished helmet. Its chain mail was old and worn, its face hollow with slash marks on the cheekbones. It was then Abel recognized the beard, the muddy brown hair that covered the Norse man's chin and extended near a foot down his chest. Abel had known only one man in his life with a beard like that: Hári. The man was as fast as a rabbit, if Abel's memory served him correctly.

A flash back to the boat. The lightning. Hári standing beside him, not fast enough to get out of the way. The lightning must have brought him here, too, though not to the same place. Hári must have been *changed* to the dead at some other point and was gathered to be here.

Gathered to fight.

To the death.

"Forgive me, brother, for I knew you well," Abel said.

Hári only stared at him. The shackles fell from his wrists and ankles. Hári charged.

Abel moved to bring his blade clean across Hári's neck, but just as he was about to do so, he withdrew and stepped to the side; Hári ran past him.

"I cannot believe you are here," Abel said.

Hári merely growled, his bloodshot eyes no longer carrying even a hint of the man Abel once knew.

A warrior's spirit was a strong one and Hári proved it by pulling his sword from its sheath.

The crowd gasped.

Abel hadn't known any of the dead to fight with a weapon.

The two Vikings ran at each other, swords slicing through the air, each ready to massacre the other. The blades clashed mid air; a shockwave zipped through Abel's arm. Quickly he dipped down, bent at the knees, and brought his soax across the inside of Hári's thigh. Blood immediately spurt out.

Still bent over, Hári brought his blade down on Abel's exposed back, the force of the blow sending him to the ground. His knuckles hit the concrete first, fingers still gripping his weapons. A dead weight suddenly plowed into his back, pressing him against the ground. A sharp pain shot through his arm and he didn't need to look at it to know Hári had ran his blade through it.

Screaming, Abel tried to pull himself out from under his former comrade. Instead, the most he could do was rock his body side to side and hope to loose him.

Searing pain lit up his pierced arm. He glanced over. Hári was chewing through it. Abel tugged and tugged, intentionally loosening the muscle and fat for the undead Viking. With a wet tear, he pulled what was left of his arm free, in turn getting him the leverage he needed to jerk out from under Hári's weight and crawl off to the side.

Hári sat on his knees, hunched over the arm, devouring the flesh off the bone. Blood trailed in a long, thick puddle from the arm over to where Abel sat off to the side, shaking from the pain.

The crowd's screams droning in his ears, all going blurry before him, Abel wondered about his mates back home and if, even now, they looked upon the deck of the *Snake of the North* to where he once stood, still wondering what happened to their friends and if they wound up overboard.

Abel plunged the tip of his sword into the ground and used it to help himself to his feet. Seemingly sensing that he did so, Hári got to his feet as well, dropped the arm and looked at him.

"Remember yourself, Hári," Abel said.

Hári charged him.

Abel brought up his sword . . . and brought it down.

21
A HARD KIND OF LOATHING

If MICK HAD a crowbar, he'd take it to his own head right now. Either that, or take the hooked end, wedge it in his eye sockets and pop his eyes out. At least that way he could claim he could no longer see the Controller and make an informed choice. Bottom line: he lost again, and still owed close to eight hundred grand. It was as if Sterpanko was somehow rigging it—even the fighters. Maybe the money didn't mean anything to Sterpanko and instead the guy who ran Zombie Fight Night was just a sick freak who enjoyed blood, guts and, well, zombies.

Like before, Mick resigned once again to just spend-spend-spend and hope for the best. No time to even hope for a payout at the end. Now it was all about staying alive and seeing the night through. Once—*if*—he got to the end of it, *then* he could focus on just getting home, seeing Anna, crawling into bed and, hopefully, waking up tomorrow morning and pretending it was all a bad dream.

If only.

"Hmph," Mick said.

"You say something?" Jack asked.

Mick shook his head. He didn't feel like talking. Even if he did, he doubted he could even find the strength to speak. It was one of those moments where the words were locked in his throat, as if the words and phrases had hit some kind of ceiling and merely bounced off and dropped back down into his stomach.

There were few times in Mick's life where he genuinely hated himself. Sure, he had moments like everyone where he wished he was someone else—but no, this was different. This was one of those moments where loathing himself was his reality, the kind of hatred where if he could step outside himself, he'd kick himself in the nuts, tell himself off and kill himself—just to make a point and hurt himself so bad out of pure, rage-filled disgust.

It was one of those moments where he couldn't believe he was himself, the one with the problem, the problem that was insurmountable, deadly and, above all things—and which made it sting even more—could have been completely avoided had he merely kept a decent level of self control.

A hard kind of loathing.

It was the kind of problem where you simply wanted to turn it off, call it a day and say good night. Except, the irony of those problems were they *couldn't* be turned off by a simple solution. This kind took an all-out war just to face the music never mind actually solving it.

He was so sick of dwelling on it. He'd been doing that all evening.

New resolution: not only did he no longer care about the money, he no longer cared about *himself.*

It was the only way to stay sane. Just write *yourself* off, call it a day and say good night.

After one more bet.

He pulled out the Controller from the seat in front him and just held it. Every few seconds his eyes would begin to drift to the screen, but he'd pull them back and force them to stare forward again past the fight cage and to the rows of seats beyond. Even the faces weren't digestible. Just blurred beige and brown circles, dotted with tiny black specks and squiggly lines.

A sharp pain sparked in his ribs and his first inclination was his muscles were spasming from the stress, but it was Jack, sticking a thick elbow into him.

"Better make up your mind, friend. Show's coming down the pike, you know?" Jack said.

"Yeah." Mick mouthed the words more than said them. He didn't have to look at Jack to know the guy knew something was wrong. He had to be careful. The betting had to stay personal. Mick cleared his throat and forced the word out again: "Yeah."

"Then get 'er done."

Mick nodded and forced himself to look at the pale blue glow of the Controller screen. At first the details of the next fight didn't even register. He had to read the notes two more times before it sunk in. You could only see the word "zombie" so many times before the death machine it represented didn't carry any weight anymore. But there was another word there that *did* carry some weight.

Mick gazed passed the Controller to his feet. He tapped his left, then his right, then his left again. He bounced the rhythm back and forth a few times as if the stalling would somehow make the decision easier. And honestly, it did. When he entered his bet, he felt better and, for the first time this evening, felt like he made the right choice.

He had to feel for the pouch in the rear of the seat in front of him because the lights had gone out before he had a chance to put the Controller back.

22
WEREWOLF vs ZOMBIES
BET: $350,000
OWING: $794,000

HER NAME WAS Ursula.

When the buzzer sounded and the lights went on, she wasn't surprised the audience readily booed and hissed at her. After all, she was only four-foot-four, a little over a hundred pounds, blonde, petite and only seventeen. Whichever dead man—slow or quick—rose from the iron ring would surely tear her to shreds.

Ursula wasn't a stranger to insults or being frequently underestimated. If anything, her home life had taught her insults and condescension was the norm. Her father kept calling her a "skank just like your mother," and her mother always brought up that if she was any more introverted, she'd turn into a hopeless toad like her father.

It was amazing what could happen to a person when you kept getting told the same things over and over again. By the time Ursula was thirteen, she had already had six boyfriends. By the time she was fourteen, she was up to ten. At fifteen, she took things to the next level with them and the back seat of a car never looked the same again.

His name had been Tom Hudlemon. Cute. Brown hair. A little extra meat on the bones, but nothing disgusting. He was known to be the kind of guy who had a new girl hanging off his arm every few weeks. He was also known for his vintage 2001 Corvette, still red and glossy after all these years. It was in this 'Vette that Ursula knew she could seduce Tom into taking things around the bases.

One night, after grabbing a couple Slurpees, the two eventually found their way onto a darkened street with very few houses left since the world fell apart and the dead were bombed to smithereens in every city. It didn't take long for Tom to set his Slurpee down and reach over to her. At first, she didn't mind, the car being dark from the lack of moonlight thanks to the thick clouds overhead. Ursula let him take hold of her, draw her close and start running his hand up her leg. Within a few seconds, the interior of the car grew lighter as the full moon above revealed itself from behind a dark gray cloud. Ursula pulled away, fearing the light being shone on the vehicle might reveal a little too much for any passersby or someone looking out their window.

Then the *heat* filled her body. It was as if her blood had been replaced with boiling water. Screaming, she jerked and twisted, one of her feet snapping up and connecting square with Tom's chin. Ursula's skin burned and when she looked down, thick hair shot forth from beneath her skin, covering her arms, hands—everything. Something sharp jabbed into her bottom lip. When she ran her tongue across it, she was shocked to find her teeth had grown exponentially.

Tom just stared at her, eyes wide, jaw open. Then the *heat* returned and all she wanted was to taste the flesh inside him.

Here, in the ring, Ursula figured it was the best way to satisfy the wolf within, something that manifested itself more and more since that night with Tom. Just last year, she was finally able to control it and transform at will, except for the nights when it was a full moon. On those nights, willpower was irrelevant and there was nothing else but the need to feed and dominate. And at least here, fighting the dead, she wouldn't be a good-for-nothin' like her parents made her out to be. In this ring, she was somebody. Somebody with a name people knew and somebody with more money than they knew what to do with.

The iron ring lit up and the dead began to rise.

Ursula got ready, one foot back, the other forward, weight distributed evenly.

The crowd's tone changed and began yipping and hollering. They were obviously cheering for the zombie because if they had seen her fight before, they'd know what she was and wouldn't have booed her earlier.

The dead man before her appeared to have been young when he died, Asian, with a slim athletic build that would make any guy envious. Even a girl. His face was open on its right side, the skin dried and leathery, folded over his nose and mouth like a flap, one eye staring out from a mess of dark red flesh, the other amidst lightly tanned skin. His eyes were red. A Sprinter.

"Ready to rock?" she asked.

The dead man didn't reply, but instead glanced down at his open torn black overshirt, bare chest and black jeans.

The buzzer sounded again and the Asian man's chains fell to the ground.

"Rock and roll," Ursula said and ran away from the Sprinter.

The crowd booed as expected.

It was all a show. Let them think one thing then do a one-eighty.

She hit the chain-link of the cage with her back and ducked when the Sprinter took a swipe at her with his nails. Left then right. Quick, quick.

Go!

Ursula turned around and climbed the chain-link until she was at the top.

The Sprinter below backed up a few steps then charged at the chain-link. The impact from his body hitting it shook all the way up the cage and Ursula nearly lost her grip. Reaching up and across from herself, she took the chain-link ceiling of the cage in her fingers and began crossing them to the other side like a pair of monkey bars.

The Sprinter jumped and clawed at the air in an attempt to catch her legs. No go.

"Ha! You suck!" she said and kept swinging across.

The Sprinter jumped again and this time snagged her sneaker. Her shoe fell to the floor. Ursula reached the other side and remained up there until—

The chain-link shook all around her. Below, to either side, were two more Sprinters. The Asian one in the middle charged at the chain-link, dove into it, and shook the cage hard, forcing her to fall.

Ursula hit the ground on all fours.

Heat filled her veins and she tore off on her hands and feet across the cement floor just as the three Sprinters attempted to pounce on her. They missed, each smacking the cement good and hard.

Her skin on fire, Ursula braced for the millions of spiky hairs that were about to burst forth from her flesh.

With a loud growl, she let loose, her muscles bursting beneath her skin, increasing in size. Fur ripped through her skin and coated her in a rich brown. She tucked her upper lip back as two long canine teeth grew on either side of her tongue.

The smell.

The dead reeked; worse than they had when she was human. Yet . . . there was an appeal there as well, a foul stench that reminded her of marked territory.

Her hands now fingered paws, she barked and

growled as dark, thick claws replaced her fingernails.

The crowd went silent.

The Sprinters before her appeared to be confused, as if wondering where the little girl who was here a moment before had gone off to.

"It's me, gents," she said, voice raw and gravelly.

The rabid dead men charged her, nothing but death and murder in their eyes. Ursula leaped over to them and pounced on one of the men's backs, ripping the fella's gray hair out with her claws then bringing her maw down on his head, biting hard and deep into his skull. With her powerful jaws, she tore out his brain, swallowed some, then spat the rest off to the side. She rode the zombie's body to the ground as he fell, then she turned to face the other two.

One of them—as white as they came with pale skin, white-blonde hair and next to no pigment anywhere else—slipped off to the side as if he had no interest in her, then suddenly came rushing at her, mouth open, red eyes like rubies against white satin.

Barking, Ursula howled and sprinted at him. She leaped into the air, paws out. She punctured his guts, tore her paws down and emptied his insides all over his legs and feet. He grabbed her shoulders, lifted her up, then brought her chest to his mouth for a bite. She swatted his temple, forcing his head to the side, and bit down into his neck, tearing out his trachea. He attempted to snap at her, but instead she nipped back, this time ripping his rotting face off the bone then returning with an even wider maw to swallow his head. She bit down on his skull. It crushed beneath her powerful jaws like a raw egg, blood and brain and bone mashing between her teeth and oozing out the sides of her mouth.

A sharp pain spiked in her hind leg. The Asian had

her foot in his mouth. With a quick snap of his head, he tore her right paw off. Ursula howled. Blood gushed from the wound.

She dove on top of him, landing square on his chest. Her weight crushed his ribs and her severed foot along with blood burst forth from his mouth. She bit down on his neck just as he did hers. Hot pain ran from her shoulder right to the back of her head and in behind her ear. A moment later warm blood snaked its way between her fur, heating her skin.

She bit harder.

And harder.

23
OF VOMIT AND MEN

THE NERVE ENDINGS in Mick's face tingled. It wasn't long until his cheeks and lips were numb. His heart beat quick and hard, the muscle inside his chest vibrating. He thought it might be a heart attack. It would be wonderful if it was, but his left arm felt fine and his chest wasn't tight, just *active*. That last one should have been a no-brainer. He saw it was a girl listed on the roster. Commonsense dictated that the undead would win. Sure, he had known tough women off and on during the Zombie War, but history had shown, physically speaking, that women were usually weaker. His bet made sense.

But he should have seen through the smokescreen. No doubt Sterpanko had thrown that girl onto the roster as a kind of red herring to throw Mick off. Even someone as sick as Sterpanko wouldn't have sent an innocent little girl into the ring with a zombie for sport. Humanity still had laws against that. Despite how twisted things had become, there was still decency out there and sending a child to fight a zombie should have been obvious to Mick as a ploy.

Now he was in the hole. Big time. And by the time the night was over, yeah, he'd be buried.

"You okay, mate?" Jack said. "You don't look so good."

Mick swallowed what felt like a ball of dry flesh at the back of his throat. His stomach spasmed and dizziness filled his head. He pitched forward, opened his mouth, and let out a solid litre of sour throw up in between his shoes. He shivered from its acidy taste: orange juice with a hint of cheese and burnt shrimp. The back of his throat went instantly dry as stomach acid scorched the tender flesh.

"Oh, dude . . ." Jack said.

Mick wiped the tears from his eyes and the gob of snot that was dangling off his nose. "I'll be . . ." His voice caught. "I'll . . . be . . . okay."

"Aw, man, that's rancid."

Several people around them stirred in their seats. Many turned around or leaned forward from the row behind him to take a look and see what was going on.

Great, now people will know something is wrong. I've violated the rules. Security's gonna come and take me away. Sterpanko's going to beat my head in and I'm doomed. Mick spat out the wad of sour goop in his mouth.

He was thirsty. He cleared his throat and sat up straight. Everyone around stared at him. Even though he'd just been close to it, the smell of the puke seemed worse up here. "Sorry," he rasped. Many folks grimaced. Mick thought he heard one guy stifle off a round of throwing up himself.

"I'm tired," Mick said softly.

Jack had a hand over his mouth and nose. "You realize many of us are going to have to move, don't you?"

Mick nodded then looked over to the old guy beside him. The old fella still sat there, staring forward, the puke not seeming to faze him. "Sorry," Mick told him.

A minute later, a security guard came to the edge of the row. "Hey, buddy, what's going on?" He sniffed the air. "Ah, that's nasty."

Jack sucked himself further back against his seat to allow the security guard room to lean over and talk to Mick. The guard obviously had no trouble singling out who the troublemaker was.

Just what I need.

"Get up. Get out." The guard thumbed toward the aisle.

Mick nodded, got up slowly, and, careful not to slip, made his way over to the guard.

"Let's go," the guard said and gripped him firmly by the biceps.

He no doubt knows who I am, Mick thought. *And if not, it won't take long for whoever ends up seeing me to inform Sterpanko. Guess it's over now. Was fun while it lasted even though I blew it big time tonight.*

He glanced back once at Jack. The big guy just remained in his seat, eyes toward the cage on the floor. Many others followed Mick with their eyes as he was escorted out of the arena proper and into the hallway beyond. From there, the security guy took him to the bathroom.

"Clean up," he told Mick.

Mick just looked at him, not sure what to make of it.

"You heard me: clean up."

"Okay." Mick went into the bathroom and immediately to the sink where he splashed water on his face several times. *Guess I gotta look my best before I say my prayers and get beaten to death.* He placed both palms on either side of the sink and stared into the basin, water dripping off his face. "I'm sorry, Anna."

"You should be."

Mick turned his head. Anna punched him in the mouth. *Where'd she—*Blood gushed from his lip. The next moment, her fist came for his face again. Then it went dark.

A spike of pain blossomed at the back of his head and something cool was against his back, its cold seeping through his clothes. He opened his eyes to find himself on the bathroom floor, staring up into the face of the security guard who had brought him to the bathroom to begin with.

"Anna!" Mick shouted. He sat up quickly. Dizziness soon took over and he fell to the side. He used his forearm to break his fall, ignored the pain in his elbow from the impact, and waited a moment for the tidal wave of blood in his brain to pass. Softly: "Anna. Where is she?"

"Get up." The guard tugged him to his feet.

"My wife. She was here. She was—" Mick's eyes hurt. His nose was on fire. "Anna."

The guard pulled him by the arm. Mick tripped. The guard yanked him up and dragged him out of the bathroom.

"Anna . . . Anna . . . she was here. She hit me. She was here," Mick said. The guard pulled him along. Mick planted his feet down, forcing the guard to stop. "Hey, I'm talking, man." The guard grimaced. "Where's my wife?" Mick pointed back in the direction of the bathroom. "Let me say this slowly so you understand: there's a woman here. She's my wife. She was in the bathroom. She hit me."

The guard pulled on his arm and dragged him a couple steps.

"Are you even listening to me?"

The guard kept pulling.

"Hey!" Mick shouted and swatted the guard in the back of the head. The guard pitched forward, regained his balance, then pulled out his baton, spun around and brought it across Mick's face.

The world spun and things went dark again.

The next thing he felt was his butt slamming into something. When his head began to clear and he slowly opened his eyes, he found himself back in his seat, his left cheekbone aching, the Controller in his lap. No puke by his seat.

"Rough time?" Jack asked. "They cleaned things up while you were gone. Still stinks though. They might have left a tad, I don't know."

"I . . . I don't—" *I don't know. I don't . . . I don't know what I saw or what's going on anymore. Anna was there. I saw her. She hit me. I'm here. In the chair. Face hurts. Blood. My blood. Anna. In the bathroom. She hit me.*

"Better place your bet, mate," Jack said. "Show's about to start."

24
SUMO vs ZOMBIE
BET: $500,000
OWING: $1,144,000

ADAMU STOOD, READY, centering himself before the lights went on and the match began. Before the Zombie War, and despite the influence of the training place he lived in, the *heya*, he had made a good living from knocking other men to the floor or out of the ring. For someone like him, thirty thousand US dollars a month was not out of the question and usually it was a bit more.

But money didn't matter now, at least, not as much. Though Sterpanko paid him, it was nowhere near what he used to make. Adamu originally thought he'd earn equal to or the same as his pre-war earnings, considering every time he stepped into the ring he was putting his life on the line. Such was not the case at Blood Bay Arena, yet Adamu had no real place to go to honor his fathers. The life of a *rikishi* was lost during the war. So far as he knew, he was the only one left though he suspected there were others out there, somewhere, practicing their art. He just wished he knew where.

The problem was he couldn't search for them even if he wanted to. Sterpanko owned him, and if he did try to travel and find others, he'd either be stopped at borders, denied air travel or, worse, made an example of to any others in Sterpanko's fighting stable that wanted a way out.

Standing tall and weighing two-hundred-fifty-six pounds, Adamu had done well in the ring. Though the rules here were different than traditional Sumo bouts, the object was the same: knock your opponent to the ground or out of the ring. But in this case, ensure they didn't get back up or get back in. Adamu had done quite well on the former. The latter was impossible unless you were gifted with unnatural strength like that Axiom-man fellow. The cage was sealed off on all sides and on top.

Even now, after many bouts here, Adamu still remembered what it was like to boldly walk into the ring with the other wrestlers, proudly wearing his *kesho-mawashi*—an elaborate, embroidered silk apron—and participate in a brief ritual before returning to his dressing room to change into his fighting *mawashi*. Nowadays, it was *mawashi* only. No prior ceremonies. No respect. Just wrestling, money, and answering the call of the fighter within.

Briefly, Adamu wondered what type of the undead he'd be battling today. He knew he'd find out soon enough.

And he did. The buzzer sounded and the house lights went on. The iron ring lit up and the dead began to rise.

A Shambler stood before him, wrists bound in chains.

Adamu didn't know him personally, but this time Sterpanko had the guts to actually put a real *rikishi* in front of him and not just some mindless, bag of dead skin and guts.

It was a Sumo.

Though the ring here was not a traditional *dohyō*, he wondered if the creature across from him even knew what a *dohyō* was anymore. Regardless, Adamu got busy stomping his legs in a *shiko* exercise to drive away any evil spirits in the ring. He mentally went through the purification ritual of rinsing his mouth with *chikara-mizu* (power water) and drying it with *chikara-gami* (power paper).

He squatted, clapped his hands, showing the dead man he had no weapons, then mentally sprinkled salt into the ring to purify it.

It was time to begin and those in the shadows controlling the bout knew it.

The buzzer rang again and the undead Sumo's chains dropped to the floor.

Adamu launched his initial charge, the *tachi-ai*, something that, in the upper divisions, he didn't normally do, but here, it was charge or die. The other Sumo seemed to be doing the same thing. They plowed into each other. The thud as healthy and dead flesh collided echoed all the way up Adamu's chest. Immediately, the zombie Sumo—Zumo?—began biting, his flappy jowls pushing into him as he tried to take a chunk of meat out of Adamu's shoulder.

Adamu shoved his head into the Zumo's, pushing with enough might to knock the dead man's giant head away from his flesh.

Quick, Adamu said to himself. With that, he jerked his chest and gut forward, bumping the Zumo back. The force was hard enough that, had this been the old days, it would have forced the Zumo to stumble out of the *dohyō* no problem. The thing with the fights now was the victor had to be the one left alive. If you died outside the cage due to a fatal wound, you were still considered the victor.

When the Zumo straightened himself, he crouched down and made a second charge. Adamu ran into him, putting all his weight behind himself like a freight train. Sweaty thick flesh slapped together. Adamu grabbed the Zumo by his *mawashi,* hoisted him a couple feet from the floor, then twisted to the side, tossing the Zumo to the ground.

The crowd cheered.

Adamu kept a straight face, leaned forward slightly, and braced himself for the Zumo's next move.

The Zumo got up, turned around and ambled toward him. Adamu charged him, this time keeping his elbows in front of his body and using them as a battering ram against the mass of gray flesh before him. The Zumo took the blow to the chest, stumbled backward, then once more regained his footing.

The two men latched onto each other, Adamu wriggling the top half of himself enough to keep his shoulders and chest away from the zombie's hungry mouth. Bodies pressed together, Adamu held firm to the decaying flesh. The two moved forward then back, then twisted in a circle as each tried to take advantage of the other.

All the Zumo cared about was a sizable snack, Adamu knew. Well, he wasn't going to let him have it.

The Zumo growled and quicker than expected adjusted its arms and used them to shove Adamu backward. His bare heels caught on the cement floor and he fell onto his behind. The Zumo charged him. Rocking to the side a couple of times and building momentum, Adamu released at the last moment and rolled over as the Zumo charged past.

He got up, crouched, then held out his hands as the Zumo ran toward him. The two latched onto each other again. Adamu squeezed his elbows against the monster's flesh, hoping the dead skin would give way and maybe his elbows could puncture the zombie and cause it to bleed. The skin, though squishy, held.

Teeth began to clamp on his shoulder. Adamu jerked himself away, denying the Zumo its chance.

Nothing more than a scrape, he thought.

He quickly grabbed on again, hoisted the Zumo up a

bit, then swung the creature over his leg and to the ground a couple feet away.

The Zumo scrambled on the ground on all fours, mouth open, its aim apparently for Adamu's shins or thighs.

Adamu let him come. Closer. Closer. And closer until the Zumo was a breath away. Adamu parted his legs and the Zumo stuck his head right between his thighs. As fast and as fluidly as he could, Adamu clamped his legs together, jumped up, then swung his legs out in front of him, crushing the Zumo's head beneath his bottom, at the same time bringing clamped hands down onto the Zumo's spine, breaking it.

A gush of cool liquid oozed beneath Adamu's thighs as the dead man's blood squirted out to either side of him.

The crowd roared.

Adamu got up, careful to keep his feet and ankles away from the Zumo just in case the creature was still alive.

The Zumo lay face down against the concrete.

Adamu kept his eye on him, and after a few moments turned his back and stepped up to the edge of the cage and stared out into the audience.

The crowd cheered. Then they cheered louder.

Suddenly, strong hands grabbed Adamu's waist from behind and something slick rubbed up against the back of his thighs. He shoved himself off the cage into the air and came crashing down on the Zumo's body about mid back, flattening the creature. He reached down, grabbed the Zumo's head under the chin and pulled up until the rotting flesh of the zombie's neck gave way, then the ligaments, then the bones.

Adamu got up, holding the head in his left hand by the hair.

He held it up for the audience to see.

25
NO ANNA

Mick HAD BARELY paid attention to the last fight. Anna was here. He *saw* her. He had the sore cheekbone and bloody lip to prove it. He wiped the sweat from his brow then put his palm to his chest to try and slow his racing heart. It had been pounding so hard since being plopped back down in his chair that the muscle was beginning to ache and he feared a heart attack.

His hands trembled. He glanced around the sea of faces in the arena for any sign of Anna. Though he doubted she'd be sitting somewhere in the stands, he couldn't help himself but look.

"She's here. She's here. I know she's here," he whispered, twisting around in his seat so he could get a good look at the folks all around.

"Got a mouse in your pants?" Jack asked.

"No. Fine. Just fine. I'm fine."

"Don't sound it."

Mick stood. "SHUT UP!"

Jack's eyes went wide. So did those of the other people seated around them.

Mick took a deep breath and sat down. "I'm sorry. I didn't mean to blow up on you like that."

The big man shrugged. "Yeah, whatever, mate. Seems to me you got a lot riding tonight. I've seen paranoid. I mean, really seen it. What you got, I don't know. Some kind of crazy, that's for sure."

"Well, that may be. I honestly don't know what I'm feeling anymore."

"Should see a doctor."

"Or a shrink."

Jack looked at him crossly. "Or an exorcist."

"Never mind." *Anna. Where is she?*

Mick stood again with the mind to take another walk to the bathroom. One stern look from the greasy security guard standing by the door to the hallway told him he'd better sit his butt down lest he get a baton placed somewhere inconvenient. Mick sat. He wiped his face and coughed.

Jack was already flipping through the screens of his Controller.

"Anything good?" Mick said without meaning to. He knew the rules.

"Shhh."

"Sorry." Mick still couldn't fathom how Sterpanko or anyone else could monitor all the conversations going on in this place.

Unless each seat was bugged.

Sterpanko was a goon, pure and simple, and the fact Mick had given him so much of his livelihood—it finally set in and what felt like a peeled grapefruit made its way from Mick's chest down into his stomach. He could even taste the sourness at the back of his throat he felt so guilty.

Where was Anna?

If I let it go, then she's walking around here somewhere somehow tied into all this. If I try and find her, I'll get my nose broke. Mick sniffed. *How are you even involved in this, Anna? I just don't—*

Jack nudged Mick with his elbow. "Better get thinking, partner. Battle's about to go down."

"Sure. Thanks." *Jack keeps reminding me to bet. I have to stay focused.* Mick pulled out his Controller and took in the details of the next bout. It looked interesting, that was for sure. This thing with Anna, though—He had to figure out a way to find her or see her somehow. He also needed to try and focus and win back as much cash as he could otherwise, whether he found her or not, he wouldn't be seeing her again after tonight.

"What do you do when the Reaper's coming for you?" he muttered, then placed his bet.

26
WRESTLER vs ZOMBIE
BET: $275,000
OWING: $644,000

THERE WERE FEW places on Earth that Shanna could be herself. The first and most immediate was at home with her husband, Steph, the second—well, the second wasn't around anymore, but it had been with her family, growing up with them, sharing meals, getting lessons—all before the Zombie War. Now they were but a memory, gone to the waves of time along with the security that came with the knowledge that despite her enormous size, she was still perceived as a woman and not some sort of man-made-lady that many thought her to be.

The last place she was comfortable was here in Blood Bay Arena, in the ring. Here she was expected to be out of the ordinary. A six-foot-four, two-hundred-and-seventy-five-pound woman? Sure, you betchya. We see those sorts of things here all the time. A muscular frame that would make a grown man think he's looking at Arnold in his prime, you say? Them's the norm around these parts. Move along, nothing to see here.

However, being a pro wrestler on Zombie Fight Night wasn't too bad a gig. Shanna got paid well enough and Mr. Sterpanko seemed to have taken a shining to her for some strange reason. Why? She didn't know. But here . . . yeah, here, she could be herself. Be *human* again and not some large woman that people pointed or children stared at. "Look, Mom, she's stronger than Daddy." Or, "Must be on the juice. Nobody gets that big naturally." That last part was a common misconception when it came to how she got to be the way she was. It *did* come naturally. Her body had polycystic ovary syndrome, and produced far more testosterone than your average female, thanks to cysts on her ovaries. Her estrogen output was just enough to cover the basics and give her the right desires God intended, but other than that, she had the body of Mr. Universe, and some unfortunate health issues to go along with it.

It first started back during puberty. Grade four for her. In gym class she noticed she was better at the games than most of the other girls. While their swings at bat during baseball sent the ball as far as short stop, hers cleared the field most of the time. She was even made starting pitcher one season of softball. Coach said her arm moved swift like a windmill and delivered a ball with the punch of a hurricane to the catcher beyond.

Soon she grew much faster than the other girls and even by grade nine she was near six feet. Some guys loved the height; others called her "beanstalk" or "oak lady." Many of those boys wound up with a black eye at the end of the day and she got consecutive trips to the principal's office in return.

Muscle-gaining came easy and she hit the weights for the first time when she was fifteen years old. Soon, she got involved in inter-school wrestling. After high school, she wrestled in the university league. After that, she turned pro and scored two heavyweight titles in the women's division then quickly suggested to the league owners they let her compete against the men. They were afraid a woman competing against a man for the title would stir up controversy, but she convinced them to utilize that to their advantage and reap the financial benefits such a scandal would cause. She took on

Thunder Guns, the reigning champ at the time, and had him pinned inside of four minutes even though it was originally planned she should throw the fight. They let her keep the title for a few weeks before firing her for disobedience. The fans thought she had merely been written out of the story.

Then the Zombie War came and after it ended, she found herself back in an industry that once destroyed her livelihood. Still, to be herself and not some freak was wonderful and she didn't mind being a part of the biz again if it meant a means to let loose some of her aggression and not have to worry about what other people thought about her.

As she stood there in the dark, she clenched her fists, then relaxed her hands and adjusted her leather corset. She double checked the long braid of her blonde hair to make sure it was in place, and she stamped her heels against the ground, psyching herself up.

She was ready. It was time to show these people what she was made of.

The buzzer sounded and the lights went on.

The iron ring lit up and the dead began to rise.

Blood Bay Arena did its best to match the zombie to the fighter, something to give the crowd their money's worth. Shanna's matches were no exception and standing before her was a hulk of a man, gray-skinned and purple-veined, wearing nothing but a pair of boxer shorts. Red gauges dotted the man's skin. It looked as if he was a seasoned fighter and the damage had been done by a werewolf or other creature. He had short, greasy black hair, and wrinkly, gray circles around his eyes. The man's hands were like baseball mitts. Unfortunately, he was a Shambler, and combining that with his appeared weight of two-hundred-fifty-or-so pounds, the guy was going to move slow.

You could end this quickly and be in a hot bath inside of ten minutes, Shanna thought. She wasn't sure if she was in the mood to give everybody a show or not, yet it would still be something sweet to see a big blonde take out a large dead man.

The buzzer rang and the dead man's chains fell to the concrete floor.

Lights shining bright above, Shanna took a quick second to say a prayer of help, then focused herself at what needed doing. The secret here, as always, was to not get bit. If you kept away from a zombie's mouth, you had an eighty percent chance of survival already. The other trick was to stay away from their *hands*. Once those slapped down on you, they dragged and pulled you in until the undead could lock their teeth around your neck or shoulder. Being near their *arms* was okay. The undead didn't really use them to reel you in. It was the hands—the grab-and-pull—that was dangerous. The other advantage was the zombies normally led with their face, mouth-first, so you knew where they were aiming for on your body and you could then avoid them.

The zombie stumbled toward her. Shanna side-stepped, forcing it to follow her in a circular pattern.

The creature lunged at her. She stepped to the side and the zombie grabbed nothing but air. She maneuvered around it so she was behind, grabbed the zombie by the waist, bent her knees, then thrust upward with all her might, throwing the zombie over her shoulder in a well-executed suplex.

Releasing him, she got up, took two quick steps so she was alongside the zombie, then cocked her elbow and put her bodyweight behind it as she plowed it into his spine, crashing down on top of him.

The crowd cheered, loving every minute of it.

Giving in to a bit of showmanship, Shanna squatted over the zombie, facing his feet, then dropped her backside onto the small of his back. With a firm grip, she took up the zombie's ankles and pulled hard, forcing the legs toward her and turning the zombie's body into a perfect U: pure Boston Crab.

Hoots and whistles filled the arena.

Shanna smiled, released the dead man, got to her feet and strode over to one side of the cage, tossing her arms up.

"Yeah? Yeah? You want more? Huh! Okay, you got it!" she growled.

More whistles.

The zombie was getting to his feet. Shanna ran over to him and stomped her foot into his ribcage, stopping him. The decayed flesh gave way and a gush of blood followed by a glop of rotting intestine poured out.

The zombie fell onto his side.

Shanna took a step away and raised a fist to the crowd.

The dead man slowly got up, shook his head as if he was trying to shake the cobwebs out, then lumbered over to her, arms outstretched, moving them up and down like flesh-made scissors.

Shanna weaved under the arms, once, twice—and on the third the zombie caught her and began pulling her in. The man's hands were rough and heavy, like lead-filled balloons, with a strength that made his fingers dig deep into her skin. She kicked at the ground, trying to push away. The zombie lost its grip for a moment but quickly re-established it. Mouth open, he pulled her in toward it.

With a swift right hook, she knocked the zombie's jaw to the side, then came back with an uppercut and landed her fist squared where the jaw met the neck. The zombie's head snapped back and she hoped the force of the blow was enough to break his neck. The zombie released her, stumbled back a few steps, then slowly brought his head forward again.

"Are you serious?" she said.

She snapped out her arm and ran at him, quickly veering to the side at the last moment and took the zombie down with a mighty clothesline.

She stomped on the zombie's back. The undead man jerked, his sudden move so unexpected that the jolt of his girth was enough to knock her off balance. She fell backward on her behind.

The crowd screamed. She thought she heard someone shout, "Look out!"

She tried to roll to the side just as the zombie grabbed her legs, but it was too late. The creature had her and was tugging at her boot, trying to figure a way around the laces and into the tender flesh beneath.

She kicked her feet as hard as she could, gave it all she had in a mad scramble to gain some distance.

"Don't get close. Don't get close," she told herself. *Getting close will kill you.*

One foot . . . two. She was free.

She ran to the other side of the cage, bounced off the chain-link, and charged straight at the zombie just as he was standing up. She leaped into the air and sent both feet into the dead man's chest. The creature slammed back against the cage on the other side. Shanna landed on her back.

A sudden woosh of dizziness overtook her and black fuzz lined her vision. A moment later and a searing pain ignited at the back of her head. It took a moment, but the two words "head" and "impact" bounced around inside her skull. Ears buzzing, she caught sight of something big and gray lumbering toward her.

A man.

A dead man.

A zombie!

Shanna rolled over to the side, face down. For a second she forgot what she was trying to do and her heart sped up in panic. Meaty hands grabbed her waist and yanked her to her feet.

Her head lolled back, then she quickly jerked it forward just as a set of yellow teeth snapped at her cheek.

Screeching, the crowd roaring for blood, pain already lighting up the back of her skull, she tossed her head back in one swift jerk and head butted the zombie, somewhere hopefully between the eyes, enough to daze him for a second.

She pressed down on the zombie's hands, releasing his hold on her.

Giving in to the whirlwind of instinct flooding through her, she stepped forward, grabbed the zombie by the neck, and forced him to bend at the waist. Then she wrapped her arms under him, jerked the dead man's body and legs up so he was inverted, pulled him up even higher . . .

. . . and let that pusbag have a Power Bomb, sending him crashing to the floor with all her might.

She stomped forward and slammed her foot down on the back of the zombie's head.

The skull cracked beneath her foot and brain oozed out like rotten banana from its peel.

27
OPTION FOUR

"I'M A GENIUS," Mick said quietly. *Thank you very much, I'm almost out.* It took everything he had to keep a smile from forming on his face.

Okay, just breathe. Brreeeaaatthhe. He let out a slow exhale.

In his peripheral, he caught Jack shifting uncomfortably in his seat.

That last one mustn't have gone so well for him, he thought. He pretended he hadn't noticed.

"I really need to go to the can," Mick said.

"Again?"

"That last visit was to wash the puke off. Besides, I got a bladder like an infant."

"Hmph. Come to think of it, actually, I gotta tinkle, too."

Mick chuckled, trying to convince any secret onlookers he was settling back in instead of wondering where the heck Anna was. He had to find her.

Jack got up. "You coming?"

"In a sec."

Jack left.

Mick needed to find his wife.

Option One: try and make a break for it past the security guard. Naw. Wouldn't work. Another would catch up to him right away and clobber him.

Option Two: try to sneak away and get back in time for the next fight and hope no one notices. But he wasn't a ninja, so that one was out as well.

Option Three: hire a ninja?

Mick shook his head, wondering where that last thought came from.

Option Four:

Mick bent at the waist and untied his boot. He flipped it over and inspected the sole. Clumps of dirt from Blood Bay's floor and a chunky sheen of puke from the incident earlier coated the bottom of his boot.

As discreetly as he could, he took a whiff of the sole. The sharp stench pierced his nostrils, the fumes enough to prime his gag reflex. Then with as wide a mouth as he could manage, he stuck out his tongue and ran it up and down the length of his boot, licking off as much of the funky gooey slop as he could. The spongy, mud-like mixture sat in a ball on his tongue. He rolled it around in his mouth a couple of times before swallowing.

Instantly, his stomach revolted and a stream of puke launched out of his mouth. Mick made sure to shake his head a little as the stuff came out so as to get it everywhere and cause an even bigger scene.

However, the old guy sitting next to him didn't seem to notice.

Mick stood hunched over, retching, when a pair of hands grabbed him by the collar and dragged him out into the aisle.

"I oughtta beat you down to a pulp, you know that?" a voice said.

Mick glanced up through watery eyes to a meaty security guard, this one not the guy standing by the door to the hallway.

The big man grabbed him under his arm and dragged him up the steps to the door, Mick's insides still convulsing all the way.

At least I'm on my way out, Mick thought. "Bathroom . . ."

"Not this time," the guard said.

Just as they passed through the door, Mick bumped into Jack.

"Hey, man, what gives?" Jack said, arms outstretched.

Mick didn't have a chance to reply as he was taken down the hallway to a metal door at the far end, up six flights of concrete steps, and was brought into another hallway, the walls lined with yellow bricks.

His stomach muscles were still contracting and little chunks were coming up again. He could barely keep his feet under him.

The guard hauled him to the room at the far end, shoved him inside the dark room, then closed the door behind them, keeping a firm hand on Mick's shoulder. A moment later, the light went on.

"Why are you doing this, Mick?" Sterpanko moved from the far side of the plainly-furnished room. There was a large window behind him overlooking the cage below. A row of four black leather chairs were positioned in front of the window. That was it. Nothing else other than gray carpeting and charcoal black-painted walls.

"Doing what?" Mick said.

"You come here, screw me over, and I by my good graces decide to give you a chance to get out of this mess and all you do is lose money, cause a scene" —he snapped up the first two fingers of his right hand— "*twice* yack all over the place—SENSELESS! You really do live like a man with nothing to lose, don't you?"

Mick swallowed, winced, and cleared his throat.

"Want to say something?" Sterpanko said.

"No. Just a cough."

"You've done enough of that already, don't you think?"

Mick didn't answer.

"I asked you a question."

The guard tightened his grip on Mick's shoulder, digging his thumb deep into the flesh.

"Yes," Mick said. "Sorry."

"You should be. And now here we are." Sterpanko pulled a cigar out of his breast pocket, stuck it in his mouth, lit it, then put the lighter back in his pocket. He exhaled a thick plume of smoke. "I've already given you the speech about what will happen if you don't perform today, so I'll spare saying it again."

Sterpanko walked over to the large window, looked down and didn't say anything. A moment later, he reached inside his coat pocket and pulled out a cordless Controller.

The guard walked Mick over to him. Sterpanko handed him the device.

Mick just held it.

"Are you going to place a bet?" Sterpanko asked.

"Do I have a choice?"

"No."

Sighing, Mick registered himself with the machine and flipped through the screens to see what the next fight held. He made his selection and handed the Controller back. "There."

Sterpanko put the device back in his pocket. "Let's see what happens."

28
BIGFOOT VS ZOMBIES
BET: $369,000
OWING: $369,000

THE FLASHES CAME only once and a while now. There used to be a time when they came quite regularly, shots of a world from long ago from a time that was no more.

The Bigfoot's mind wasn't as underdeveloped as most people thought. His name was Stalla. Though not his pack's Alpha Male, he most definitely was one of the fiercest. He *knew* that much. Reason and process-of-thought wasn't beyond him either. He prided himself on that and reflected on it often. Sometimes, for amusement, he'd pretend he didn't understand what Steer-payn-koh and those with him were saying, or would feign just enough understanding to comply with what they wanted but only half-heartedly. It seemed to appease them enough.

Those flashes. Bright images of hairy beasts, large hands, pushed-in noses and glorious fangs. His people. His kind.

Of which he was the last.

The *muptigs*, as his people referred to them, had caused so much trouble before, building cities out of the fruits of the woods, killing trees just to harvest their strong interiors beneath the bark. The *muptigs* were what forced Stalla and his family to retreat further into the trees. It was a tradition—though Stalla had trouble recalling from where—for one to retreat deeper into the forest at the first sign of a *muptig*. He only knew two things in regards to those smaller and balder versions of themselves: retreat into the forest; cover your head while doing so. The stories passed down from his grandfather said that the *muptig* were able to shoot hard things from their hands, so fast and with so much force that those hard things would penetrate your skull if you weren't careful. They were even strong enough to make your blood run freely on the ground and end your life.

It was the *muptigs'* ability to shoot hard things from their hands that created the fear inside the world of the Bigfoots. It was the *only* thing they feared.

Until that day when the *muptigs* came, this time appearing differently than before. Their skin was lighter, wounded, and their foul smell was even worse than their original scent. These *muptigs*—*thwellers*, as they became known amongst the Bigfoot—did not shoot hard things from their hands. To a degree, they were like the Bigfoot and devoured their prey with their teeth, sometimes using their claws to reel their meals in.

Stalla always believed in the idea that *muptigs* would be afraid of his kind if they were presented to them. Everyone in his tribe thought he was crazy. But he was right because one night—before the *thwellers* arrived—a *muptig* was moving through the woods, appearing to be searching for something. Stalla had stepped out from behind a tree and startled the *muptig*. The *muptig* screamed and on wobbly legs tried to run away only to trip and fall to the forest floor. Stalla had braced himself for the impact of a hard thing from the *muptig's* hands, only to find that nothing came from the *muptig's* hands at all. Stalla left that *muptig* there in the dark and returned to his tribe with the news of what he'd done. No one believed him, except one—the tribe's leader and Alpha Male, Yugta.

To show the leader that *muptigs* were actually harmless, the two set out the next night in search of one. The night went on and no *muptigs* were found. However, after wandering through the forest all night and just before the sun came up, Stalla saw one and called Yugta over. He told Yugta to stay behind the bush and watch him go up to the *muptig* and scare it. Being the Alpha Male of the group, that didn't sit well with Yugta and he instead pushed past Stalla and strode into the path of the *muptig*. The *muptig* didn't scream, as Stalla expected. Instead, it merely looked quizzically at Yugta, as if trying to process that which was before it. Then, with a quick jerk of its body, it jumped onto Yugta and sunk its teeth into his neck. Dark streams of blood arced from the wound and stained the green and brown of the forest trees and bushes. Yugta fell and the *muptig* kept eating.

Stalla watched from behind the trees. He so desperately wanted to howl over losing his friend, but instead found himself pinned with fear and unable to move. This wasn't a *muptig* like the other night. This thing eating his friend was something else. Some kind of . . . *thweller*, an "eater."

When he returned to his tribe, they were already under attack, *thwellers* everywhere, chasing and eating and cutting open all those he loved.

Stalla ran.

Now, in the dark of the arena, a flash of blood-coated hair danced before his eyes.

A sound droned overhead. The lights went on.

Blue light lit a circle on the floor and a *thweller* began to rise.

This *thweller* had eyes like blood, pale skin, and pure hate upon its face.

The joyous screams of *muptigs* filled Stalla's ears.

A loud noise droned again and that which bound the *thweller* fell to the floor.

The *thweller* moved instantly, charging straight toward him.

Stalla took a giant step to the side, hoping the *thweller* would run on past him and he could attack the creature from behind. Instead, the *thweller* matched his movement and went to the left with him, plowing mouth first into Stalla's big and hairy chest. The monster's mouth tried to work its way through the mats of hair, searching for flesh. He grabbed the *thweller* on either side of the head and yanked the creature off, the *thweller* bringing a mouthful of thick brown hair between its teeth along with it.

This was going to be easy.

The *thweller* grumbled and groaned as Stalla held either side of its head, keeping the creature's body from touching the ground. Then, using his chest and shoulder muscles, Stalla squeezed his hands together. There was a split second of resistance, then the *thweller's* head burst open at the top, brain and blood shooting out of it like a jam-packed pumpkin. Its mouth slowly moved up and down, as if it realized that its life had just ended, yet even then it still yearned for one last taste of solid meat.

Stalla dropped the body at his feet then stepped on it toward the creature's legs, his massive weight pulverizing the corpse like he did that coyote that one time, leaving only a sack of skin filled with mushed meat behind.

Stalla raised his massive hands and arms skyward, howling at the audience as they cheered. Others in the crowd made a different sound, one low and long: "Booooo." Stalla growled.

Soon the droning hisses and low booing from the crowd blended with wild cheering and, eventually, was replaced. Stalla searched the cage for the source of their amusement. Rising out of the iron ring stood three more *thwellers*, two males and one female. Each had a head of brown hair. One of the *thwellers* had hair on its face, the other two did not. Blood coated their torn clothes, all of them wearing white. Stalla was amazed that the blood remained splotched clearly in its place, bringing a sharp contrast to the white of their clothing. It was almost beautiful.

This was a new trick. So far in his career battling in the cage, the enemy had only been offered to him one at a time, and each of the *thwellers* that stood before him were the aggressive sort, the ones that ran instead of walked. The ones that charged instead of wobbled toward you like some kind of half-asleep beast.

The moment the three *thwellers* rose so their feet were level with the cage floor the chains were released and all of them made a mad dash for Stalla. He threw out his big hairy arms to either side and ran at them, slamming his biceps into two of their necks, forcing them to fall backward to the floor. The third—the female—just simply rushed past. Stalla kept her in his peripheral and spun around on his leathery-soled feet and met her head-on as she sped toward him, growling and shrieking like an eagle in the night.

Stalla slammed his palms down on the cage floor and used them as leverage and vaulted himself into the air, coming at her feet-first. The sharp claws at the end of his toes connected squarely with her face, two of his toes lodging themselves deep in her eyes. He jerked his legs back, ripping her eyes from their sockets, doing so accidentally shoving his heel into her mouth. Her teeth clamped down. Stalla howled, then yelped when she tore the bottom of his foot away as he fell to the floor.

Ignoring the pain, he stood up and met the two males

that had now gotten to their feet. In an instant he swiped a gigantic paw at them and cleaved off one of the *thweller's* faces. He then leaped away from the second as it came at him, jaws snapping, and finished the female off by digging his claws into her skull, then peeling the bone back like de-boning a fish. Brain and blood glopped out of her cranium and she hit the floor.

A male *thweller* latched onto Stalla's back and bit hard and deep to where his neck met his shoulder. The sharp sting of his hair being torn from his skin was quickly masked when the flesh beneath the hair gave way and blood and meat started to splash out.

He reached over his shoulder, grabbed the *thweller* just underneath its jaw with both hands, and flipped the creature over his shoulder. The *thweller* hit the concrete floor with such force that its skull cracked on impact, blood immediately beginning to pool around it. Stalla bent down and opened his mouth wide and bit off the *thweller's* face, opening its skull, then stood and spat the bloody skin and flesh and shards of bone toward the audience. Most of them cheered. A few hissed.

Stalla didn't care.

The zombie didn't move.

Suddenly the pain in his heel ignited as if he had been bitten afresh and he had no choice but to *not* step on it otherwise his leg would surely fold beneath him.

The faceless zombie tugged on his hand as if trying to free a stray branch from a rushing stream. Stalla jerked his fist toward himself, bringing the *thweller* along with it. The *thweller* had its mouth open and when its head connected with Stalla's, it took a bite out of the Bigfoot's lip. Blood sprayed on both of them. Stalla growled and dug his claws deep into the *thweller's* chest and pulled out anything that would quickly give: bone, meat, veins, heart—glory.

The *thweller* didn't seem to mind and kept snapping its jaws.

Blood continued to gush from Stalla's wounds and his vision began to go blurry. The only thing he was certain of at the moment was the pain and the snapping jaws in front of him.

He fell to his knees, dragging down the *thweller* with him. His vision grew darker around the edges and the inside of his head felt lighter and lighter, as if something was removing the bones from beneath his skin. He didn't know what to call the sensation but wanted more than anything to just sleep.

Snapping jaws.

Stalla couldn't let it win.

He reached into the creature's mouth. The *thweller's* teeth bit through his paw. He didn't care. He teetered backward, fell over, the *thweller* now resting on top of him, its blood cool and soaking through the hair on his chest and stomach.

Stalla turned his paw over inside the *thweller's* mouth so his claws dug into its roof, and with one swift-yet-effort-filled motion, jerked his hand upward, ripping off the top of the *thweller's* head. The creature fell lifeless on top of him.

Stalla's vision darkened.

The crowd cheered somewhere distant.

This was for Yugta.

29
THIS IS NEW

MICK STOOD THERE, heart pounding, his mind playing the last few moments of the fight over and over. A draw? Mick couldn't recall the last time that happened, if at all. But he also hadn't seen every single zombie fight either.

He turned to Sterpanko. "Now what?"

The man pressed his lips together and for the briefest of moments, Mick thought he didn't know what to do. Yet, of course, Mick knew that wasn't the case. If Sterpanko was anything, he was smart and calculating. He was the type of guy who had Plans A through D for everything. Surely the scenario of a draw had been taken into account when Zombie Fight Night was first created, especially given the contenders.

Sterpanko reached for the Controller and began tapping buttons. A few moments later, he stopped. "That was quite a bet, Mick. If you had won, we'd be even."

"I *did* win, though. I bet on Bigfoot. The zombies are dead. All *four* of them."

"Yes, but Bigfoot is dead, too, isn't he?"

"So if that happens, rules say last one alive is the victor."

Sterpanko eyed him coolly. "We continue."

"What?"

Sterpanko narrowed his eyes.

"You're serious?"

"I don't joke, Mick. You ought to know that by now."

"So that last fight—"

"Doesn't count."

Without thought, Mick lunged at him. In a flash, the security guard was at Sterpanko's side. Another instant later and Mick's face lit up with bright red pain. He hit the floor and looked up at Sterpanko. The guard beside him rubbed his fist.

"Seems you got a hard head on you. Marcus here usually doesn't wince when taking care of business for me," Sterpanko said.

Marcus took a step toward Mick then glanced back at Sterpanko as if waiting for instruction.

Sterpanko put up a hand. "Leave him be." He pulled a handkerchief from his breast pocket and tossed it down to Mick. "Wipe your face. You're getting blood all over the carpet."

Mick pinched his bloody nose with the handkerchief and held it tight.

From out of the shadows behind Sterpanko, a familiar figure stepped forward.

"Anna!" Mick said then coughed.

She put a hand on Sterpanko's shoulder.

"Is he out?" she asked him.

Sterpanko shook his head. "Not yet. Came close on that last one, though."

"Figures," she said, giving Mick a cold glare.

"Anna, what are you doing here?" Mick said. "It *was* you I saw. You hit me. You f—"

Marcus delivered his boot under Mick's chin, snapping his mouth shut and sending him toppling backward so he lay on the floor.

"Can't have you swearing in front of the lady," Marcus said.

"Go to hell."

He heard Marcus take a step forward then Sterpanko said, "It's okay."

"Told you he couldn't deliver," Anna said.

Mick felt around his head and torso for the handkerchief that had fallen out of his hand. He located it beside his shoulder then put it against his bleeding nose and mouth. "How could you, Anna?" he said through the cloth. "How could you?"

She came close and knelt down beside him. She took his hand in hers. When she spoke, her voice was like the calm after a storm. "You ruined us. You took what was ours and squandered it. You put your addiction above you and I." Her tone changed and Mick knew she was fighting back tears. "I wanted to forgive you. I love you, and I did forgive you. But it just got worse. I didn't know what you owed. I thought maybe it was a few hundred dollars. Instead you deprived us of nearly a million. One. Million." She squeezed his hand. Tears were pooled in her eyes but they did not leak. "And you know what? It's not even about the money. It's about you risking to destroy us after those we loved were destroyed. After all those people we saw killed when the dead ruled our planet. After all that madness, you took it a step further and gambled with life. *Our* lives. And you lost."

The tears came. Anna kept quiet for a few minutes as she sobbed.

"I'm sorry, sweetie, I truly am," Mick said.

She sniffled. "So am I, so much so I thought I could get Tony to forgive the debt."

Wait. "What do you mean 'get'?" He watched her closely. She glanced at Sterpanko. The man gave her a gentle smile then turned his cool-as-death eyes onto Mick.

His breath caught. Tears gushed forth. "NO!" he screamed. "NO, NOT ANNA, NO!"

He cried.

She let go of his hand.

"How—how could you?" he said. "I thought it was just you and me, always you and me."

Anna shook her head amidst the tears. "It was. Then it was just *you*. It's your fault, Mick." She stood and walked back to Sterpanko.

"No . . . please, no. Not him. Not you. I'm sorry. I'm so sorry."

"Enough," Sterpanko said.

Marcus walked over to Mick and jerked him to his feet by the arms. Mick's head swam from the sudden shift in position. A violent shove in between his shoulder blades sent him stumbling toward Sterpanko and Anna. He looked at his wife. He noticed she wasn't wearing her ring anymore. A sharp pain jabbed his heart, settled, boiled and exploded.

He had nothing to lose now. Nothing.

"Thank you, my dear," Sterpanko said and gave her a peck on the cheek.

She gave him a warm smile then walked off, not even looking at Mick once.

This wasn't the woman he married. Anna—whoever she was now . . . . He couldn't even form the thought. All he knew was that it was over.

Just like him.

He swung out and delivered a swift hook to Sterpanko's jaw. The next thing he knew something struck the back of his knees then a split second later the side of his head. He hit the floor, resting on his shins. He touched his ear and pulled away a pair of bloody fingers..

Concussion.

"Kill me," Mick said.

"Nice shot," Sterpanko said. "I'll give you that. As I mentioned, I'm a fair man."

"Bullsh—"

"Ta ta ta. Play nice."

Mick didn't care about the handkerchief anymore. Most of the bleeding had stopped anyway. As if it mattered at this point. "All right, you win," he said quietly.

"I already knew that before we started."

"Then kill me and get it over with."

Sterpanko went on as if he never heard him. "But as I said, I'm a fair man. That last fight ended in a draw. Normally the winnings would be split fifty-fifty, but what we're doing here today isn't normal."

Mick just shook his head. It was hard to believe what he was hearing yet Sterpanko was a snake so it wasn't surprising either. Man of fairness? As if. Fair to him, maybe, but most certainly not to anyone else.

Anna. I love you, Anna. And you betrayed me. Tears leaked from his eyes anew. *But I betrayed you first.*

"One more fight, Mick. Just one more," Sterpanko said.

Strong hands brought Mick to his feet again. He wanted to snap his elbow back and deliver it straight into Marcus's gut, but he didn't. It wouldn't get him anywhere except maybe . . . dead? With a smirk he twisted to the right, his elbow tight against his body. Large hands behind him caught the elbow. Mick spun around, bringing about his left fist for a hook into Marcus's head.

The blow was stopped.

Mick's mouth fell open.

A familiar face stared back at him.

30
TWO OF A KIND

"Hello, friend," Jack said.

"Hey, Jack," Mick said.

The two just stared at each other. It looked like Jack was going to say something, the words bubbling somewhere beneath the surface of that big head of his. Mick had no idea what the man would say. Or what he *could* say. Mick supposed that it kind of made sense the big fella was here.

"So this whole time, what, you were supposed to keep an eye on me?" Mick asked.

Jack nodded. "Just needed to make sure you played by the rules."

Well, we didn't do that one hundred percent, now, did we? Mick thought. "Suppose I told Sterpanko that you let me—"

"No."

And that was all it took. Behind Jack's gruff exterior, a light briefly shone then began to dim. His face said it all. Sterpanko was using him, too. Mick knew that *look*. He'd seen it in his own mirror many times on those sleepless nights where he tried to find counsel in his reflection. Jack was in deep with Sterpanko as well and his family was under threat.

"I'm sorry, Jack," Mick said.

"Me, too."

"Wish we could have had more time."

"Not me." Jack winked.

"Either way."

"Yeah."

"I'm sorry, man."

"I know. I'm sorry, too."

Mick turned to Sterpanko. "What now?"

The man clasped his hands together then pointed at him with both index fingers. "One more fight."

"And Jack?"

Sterpanko didn't even look Jack's way. "Don't worry about him. He and I have our own arrangement."

Mick glanced back at Jack. The man's face was ashen.

He's going to kill you and you're just standing there?

Mick surveyed the room. It was just him, Sterpanko, Jack and Marcus.

"When's the next bout?" Mick said over his shoulder.

"Soon," Sterpanko said. "Better pick up your Controller."

"And Jack?"

"I said, never you mind."

Mick held out his hand to Jack. "Awkward but fun, huh?"

"Yeah, who would have thought it?"

"Not me. But you're a good man, 'kay?"

"Used to be."

"Still are."

"Your opinion."

"Okay, that's enough," Sterpanko said.

"Do you really want to die today?" Mick asked Jack.

"Yeah, just like any other. You?"

Anna was gone. Everything was gone. Sterpanko was going to win either way. "Yeah."

The two men exchanged stares as if reading each other's thoughts.

"Then let's get to it," Jack said.

Mick headed for Sterpanko; Jack for Marcus.

It didn't take more than a couple of swift punches to

the face to knock Sterpanko down. Mick glanced at Jack. It appeared Jack had dove on top of Marcus and was now straddling his chest, delivering blow after blow into the man's face.

"Come on, let's go!" Mick shouted.

Jack gave one last quick shot to the guard's face then got off him. He and Mick ran for the door.

Thunder rocked the room when Mick's hand touched the door handle. He turned around to see Jack behind him, a dark red rose blossoming on his chest. Just behind him, Sterpanko held a gun out.

"Go," Jack said and fell to his knees.

"I can't leave you."

"I'm already dead." He winced and let out a grunt. "You're not. Go."

Sterpanko began his walk toward them. "Hand off the handle, Mick."

His fingers gripped the handle harder for some reason. Panic, maybe. He had to force himself to let go.

"That's it. Nice and easy," Sterpanko said, gun still aimed at him. When the man was almost upon him, he added, "One more fight, Mick. One more. Win or lose. No draw this time."

Then it *was* over. Mick looked at Jack. The big man lay face down on the carpet.

Sterpanko drew closer. The security guard groaned somewhere in the background.

"Now, Mick," Sterpanko said.

Mick raised his hands in surrender and slowly walked toward him.

A moment later, Sterpanko suddenly dropped from his line of sight. The next thing Mick knew, Jack was on top of Sterpanko, delivering feeble punch after feeble punch.

When Jack spoke, it was a cross between a whisper and a cough. "Run."

"Thanks, Jack," Mick said, and with tears in his eyes, turned and ran out of the room.

He hit the hallway beyond. Gunshots rang behind the door. He wanted to go back in and see if Jack was all right. Yet, there was no telling who had been shot. He hoped it was Sterpanko.

Mick tore off down the hallway and searched for a way out.

It didn't take long before security guards were on his tail.

31
THE CORRIDOR

MICK STUMBLED THROUGH each step, the toils of the day seeming to saturate every blood cell in his veins.

"Just hit the door," he said to himself softly. *Wait.* The guards at the front doors must have been alerted to his escape by now. If he went for the doors, he'd surely be caught. The back? Was there even a back door to this place?

Whatever, he thought and pumped his legs as fast as he could, weaving in and out between the people who were not in the arena in search of stale hot dogs, cold beer and maybe a T-shirt or two.

"Hey!" a guard shouted behind him.

"Somebody stop that guy!" shouted the other.

Ignore them. Keep running, Mick told himself. He glanced over his shoulder. The guards were about ten meters back. No matter how hard he dug his heels into the linoleum floor, attaining more speed was impossible. But there was no giving up. If he was going to go down, he was going to go down fighting. In brief reflection, Mick thought it strange that earlier tonight he didn't care at all about the outcome of the evening. Now, faced with life or death—life mattered, and if he was to die, he was going to die *living.*

He looked back over his shoulder once more and when he faced back front, he rammed smack into a hefty woman, middle-aged with a gold-yellow perm. The two went tumbling head over heels. Mick thought he heard something crack as he went over with her except he didn't feel a thing in his body. *She* must have broken something.

"So sorry," he said quickly as he scrambled to his feet. The guards were nearly upon him.

Panting, he made a sharp turn to the left, took the five steps down in a single leap, landed in a crouched position—then kept running.

He heard the frantic footfalls of the guards taking the stairs behind him.

There was a gray door on his left. Mick turned again, ran for it, then yanked it open. He pulled it closed behind him. He didn't know if the guards saw him go in here or not. It wasn't worth hanging around to find out.

Mick jogged a few steps forward and found another set of stairs that led down to a white-painted brick hallway below. He took the steps, stood in the hall for a second and looked left and right. Both directions appeared the same: white walls, a few gray doors off to either side, each end of the hallway ending in perpendicular hallways, also white-bricked and gray-floored.

He went right, somehow in his mind thinking the rear of the building was somewhere in that direction. He wasn't completely sure, though.

Mick ran. No sooner had his legs been pumping for a few seconds did a figure appear at the end of the hallway. He didn't know who it was. The only thing he was sure of was that it wasn't a security guard.

He skidded to a stop, spun around, and bolted in the other direction.

More footfalls echoed in the cement-enclosed hallway. The weird part was they were coming from somewhere ahead.

He glanced over his shoulder.

A being with white skin, white hands with claws and a blood-red cloak zipped through the air toward him like a jet out of control.

Screaming, Mick ran as fast as he could. At the end of the hallway before him, a couple of security guards appeared though Mick was pretty sure they weren't the same ones from just a few minutes back. It didn't matter. He was trapped and was already past the door with the stairs where he first entered this hallway. There was no doubling back.

"Crapcrapcrapcrapcrap . . ." The words rolled off his tongue like boulders down a hill.

His shoulders suddenly seized up and multiple spikes of pain raced through them as well as his arms. He was brought to a halt. Glancing at his shoulders he saw white hands on either side, the red of his blood clashing against the sharp sallow nails digging into his flesh.

Movement was impossible. Whatever demon had him caught from behind wouldn't let him move.

"One more fight," the thing behind him hissed.

The security guards caught up to them.

With a growl, the creature threw Mick forward and into the guards' arms.

Mick took in the beast. He knew that facial structure: the pronounced forehead, the wrinkled skin, pale as all get out, the bold cheekbones, that dash of stark white hair on top. Though the creature didn't have his giant sunglasses on, Mick knew it was the old man that had been sitting motionless beside him during this evening's fights. He didn't know what the old guy was—a vampire, maybe—and it became clear that he, like Jack, was meant to keep an eye on him.

The creature stood before him, each breath it took seeming to heave his chest up and down with rage. The old man's eyes were bright white, with red irises and golden-yellow pupils. The man didn't blink.

"I want . . . to . . . drink," the old man said. His voice was precise, each word enunciated perfectly as if a science.

"No," one of the guards said. "This man is for the boss. Thank you for your service. You will receive your payment in full as promised."

The old man grimaced then bore all his teeth, eyes wide and bright like an inferno. The vampire lashed out at the security guard, the old man's claws slicing the guard's forearm off. The man howled, and immediately cradled his arm. Mick wondered if he should take the opportunity to make a break for it.

The next instant, the vampire came at Mick. The other guard jumped in front, pounced forward and took the vampire down to the floor with him. A quick flip of the bodies and the vampire was on top. Quickly, the old man made fast work of biting into the guard's neck.

Blood gushed and sprayed. Mick could only wonder if there was more than one set of teeth inside the vampire's mouth for it seemed a few litres of blood were suddenly released from the man's body all at once.

Something whistled past his ear and a silver projectile protruded from the vampire's back on the left side.

The vampire jumped to his feet and spun around in one fluid motion, hands palm forward, claws curled, mouth wide, revealing two rows of teeth. The old man hissed and dove into the air, heading for Mick. Another whistle, and the vampire was quickly blasted backwards. He hit the floor, the silver spike that had been in his back slammed through into his chest the rest of the way, a brand new one sticking out of his heart.

The old man kicked and screamed profanities as his skin boiled and thick smoke rose off him. Then he melted away, nothing but gooey skin left behind amidst the red cloak.

Mick turned to the guard on the floor, his body prone, arm outstretched with some kind of large gun in his remaining hand. Blood was pooled around the body. The guard shook.

"Thank you," Mick said.

The guard went limp, dead.

Mick glanced up and down the hallway. "Go," he told himself and began to run.

Just then another set of guards appeared at the end of the corridor, guns raised.

"Don't move!" one shouted.

Mick raised his hands. *So close.*

The guards caught up to him.

"What happened here?" said the bigger of the two.

The other guard grimaced and gave Mick a stern look. A moment later his baton came out and all Mick saw was a blur of black heading for between his eyes.

32
ALL BETS ARE OFF

IT WAS PITCH black and Mick didn't need a light on to tell him where he was. His ears told him everything: he was in the main arena—in the cage.

One more fight, was what Sterpanko told him. He just never thought the fight would be his own. How Sterpanko could even get away with this was beyond him. Was the man's power limitless, or was he just good at pulling a blind one over everybody?

Mick's heart pounded in his chest. Watching the fights from the stands or from the couch at home was one thing. Here, in Blood Bay Arena, enclosed in a cage—he wasn't surprised when he found his throat sand-dry and had a hard time swallowing.

His legs were like Jell-O; his palms sweaty.

I am not a fighter, he thought. *A couple punches here and there, sure, but this? This is something different. This is* —the thought struck him like a kick between the legs—*life or death.*

Time seemed to slow here in the dark. He wondered if the other fighters felt the same way as they waited for their opponent to appear.

"Those guys are trained," he whispered. "Fighting is what they do." Yet a part of him felt that no matter how tough you were, fear was still there, lurking in the veins, always operating on the principles of "what if?" and "just in case."

Anna did this: his being here; his impending death; Sterpanko willing to kill him. Even that last part made more sense now. Sure, the man was ruthless and probably didn't give a crap about Mick's life . . . but at the same time now had a reason to want him dead other than for money: Anna. How long they had been together or even planned to take him out, he didn't know. As well, Sterpanko's almost *softness* in terms of Mick's case also kind of made sense. Perhaps he was supposed to just get knocked off for non-payment and that would be that? Maybe Anna had convinced Tony Sterpanko to see if Mick could earn the funds back? There was no way to know and, right now, Mick really didn't even want to know.

Tonight . . . tonight he lost everything, even a man who, though not a friend, took a bullet for him and charged him to run. Tears welled up in Mick's eyes when he realized he couldn't even do that right.

"I'm sorry, Jack," he said softly. "And, Anna? I don't know what to say to you anymore. What you did—" He hated it when the words didn't come and even now they wouldn't form. Emotion overload.

Life sucked. Good thing it'd be over soon.

The iron ring on the floor lit up.

Wrong order, Mick thought. *The lights go on first. Obviously, this change is for me.*

Some in the crowd cheered and whistled; others murmured.

The dead began to rise.

The zombie stood on the platform, bound at the wrists, its face and body concealed mostly in shadow, the blue light only shining on the thing's legs.

Mick wondered if he was expected to play by the rules. The thought of just running up to the creature right now and taking it out crossed his mind, but if he did that, yeah, he'd be dead for sure.

The lights went on. The buzzer sounded. The crowd roared.

Mick's heart sank.

The dead man before him . . . it was Jack. The bullet mark on his chest was still there, his clothes saturated in blood. Another bullet hole was on his neck. That was where he must have been shot when Mick left the room.

"Dude . . ." Mick said.

Jack's restraints fell to the floor and he fixed his red eyes on Mick.

The enormity of it—Jack, a zombie. Not long ago the two were sitting side-by-side, watching the fights. Now . . . he was a walking dead man. How could—then it all made sense.

Zombies. The world. The war. The fights. The evil. And now Jack.

Jack was a zombie. Jack only died twenty or so minutes ago. The only way people became zombies after the attacks was if one bit them. Sterpanko, Marcus—they were human last he saw.

Sterpanko.

He was behind it all.

Mick shook from the revelation and had to force his legs to move beneath him as Jack charged at him. Mick ran around the cage, Jack chasing him, the crowd beyond booing and laughing.

Who else knew? Was it all him or—Mick dropped to the ground and crunched up into a ball. Jack plowed into him with his legs and went tumbling over him. Mick grunted with the impact, got up, and ran the other way.

"I have to tell somebody," Mick said. He ran to the cage wall, gripped the chain-link and shook it with all his might. "Hey! Listen! It was Sterpanko! It was Sterpanko!" The roar of the crowd drowned him out.

Mick turned around. "Ahh!" He moved to the side and Jack crashed into the cage.

"Jack, I don't want to do this, man," Mick said. "Can you hear me? Is it still you? What about your—" He was about to say, "What about your family?" but choked on his own words when an image of Anna flashed before his mind. Was she watching this? Was she *behind* throwing him to the dead so that she and Sterpanko could live happily ever after? No way. He still thought she was the one who persuaded Sterpanko to let him try and earn back what was owed. If he was going to die tonight, he wanted to go out thinking the best of her . . . and the worst of himself.

Jack came for him. Mick took careful note to avoid Jack's hands and teeth. He put his hands up and balled them into fists. As hard and as fast as he could, he drove his fists into Jack's face. One-two. One-two. Fast. Like lightning. Jack's nose burst with blood. The zombie growled, nothing but rage contained in the shell of a big man who wasn't as bad as Mick first thought him to be.

Jack swatted Mick across the arm, knocking his hand down and sending him tumbling to the ground. Mick rolled across the floor, trying his best to ignore the jolt from the impact and the bruises he already felt forming.

He lay there, panting, sweaty, blood moistening the skin on his shoulder. Jack must have cut him with his nails.

"You can't stay down here," Mick said to himself. *He's not Jack anymore. You know that. Get up. All bets are off. Time to get it done, and if I die, I die giving it all I got!*

Mick pushed against the floor. The crowd cheered. Jack was already upon him, jaws snapping. Mick twisted his body and slammed his elbow into Jack's mouth just as the big man was about to clamp down on his neck. Jack growled at the impact. Mick noticed a tooth fly from the man's mouth.

Kicking his legs, trying to loosen Jack's grip, Mick twisted to the other side and shot his other elbow into Jack's face.

The force was enough to make Jack drop him. Mick hit the ground running and got as much distance as he could.

Jack brought his palms to the floor then charged at him like a lion, propelling himself forward with all fours. Mick tried to move out of the way and managed a step to the side before Jack quickly altered course and dove into the air and collided with him. The impact from Jack's heavy body was like getting nailed with a bag of sand. Mick coughed out the air from his lungs and was having a hard time trying to regain his breath.

Jack dug his nails into Mick's side. At first there was only profound pressure, then Mick heard the squishy *pop* of his flesh giving way and Jack's fingers invading his body.

"No! Anna! Jack! Help!" The words were pure instinct.

Heart racing, his gut going numb, the warmth of blood beginning to flow, Mick brought his face down and he latched onto Jack's ear with his teeth. Jack growled. Mick jerked his head back, ripping the ear off Jack's head. Blood oozed from the wound.

Mick spat out the ear—Jack's blood still tasting like copper, still warm, even though he had been expecting something else, perhaps something tangy and sharp—then just as quickly, he met Jack's chomping jaws head on. The two locked mouths; Mick's upper teeth over Jack's top lip, his bottom teeth digging into Jack's uppers, forcing their way to the roof of Jack's mouth. Jack clamped down on Mick's bottom teeth, Jack's lower teeth splicing through the flesh beneath Mick's chin.

Blood gushed up and to the sides in wild arcs. Some got in Mick's eye, blinding him. He bit down with all he had, refusing to let go.

Jack's hands pulled out from his sides.

Mick's body relaxed, as if in relief. Then suddenly he felt . . . lighter, as if his mid section was floating away. Something mushy and wet slipped along his sides.

He felt the grip of his bite beginning to loosen. He fought it and brought his hands up and pummelled them against Jack wherever there was an opening. Jack shook his head, tossing Mick with his mouth, forcing him to let go of his clamp on Jack's face.

Mick hit the cold floor on his back, nothing but blood around him in his peripheral.

The crowd went silent.

Jack growled and rushed toward him.

Mick closed his eyes as the lights went out.

EPILOGUE
WHAT GOES AROUND . . .

IT WAS LATE. The crowds had gone home nearly an hour ago. Anna stood inside the cage, the house lights overhead casting a burning yellow glow on the cement. The parts where it hit the blood were a deep orange.

With arms crossed, she fought back the tears as she stared at the long bloodstain on the ground that was once her husband, bits of flesh and hair, teeth and bone spackling the cement like bad stucco. Though not all of the remains were Mick's, she almost felt as if she could pick out his because she knew him so well.

Knew, she reminded herself and her heart stung. Their marriage wasn't supposed to end like this. 'Til death would they part, sure, but death wasn't supposed to come as it did tonight.

"My fault," she said.

At the time, when she snuck away that one night and cut a deal with Sterpanko, fiery hate for Mick for what he'd done drove every action and every word. Now—now she didn't know if she was still angry or not. It seemed as if Mick's death was the water that put that hating fire out.

She took a few steps back when hot red water splashed against her toes, soaking through the gaps in her high heels and burned her skin.

"Gah!" she said as her foot folded beneath her and her ankle was rubbed hard against a shard of bone, cutting her open.

The small Chinese man in the dusty blue jumpsuit didn't seem to see her as he sprayed out the cage.

"Hey, watch it!" she said. "Ow."

He merely looked up at her, nodded with a smile, then got back to spraying, the steam from the hot water beginning to fill the cage. There was a foot-square drain sloped off to the side, the grill wide enough where it needed to be to allow all the bits of gore and bone to fall through no problem.

Her foot throbbed. Probably sprained. She did her best to stand on it, swallowed the pain, and ignored the cut and burn. She deserved this. This was part of a self-imposed penance she planned to institute starting now.

She allowed her eyes to follow the flow of the water as this nameless stranger in the cage with her washed what was left of her husband away.

This was Zombie Fight Night. This was what Mick loved.

This was what killed him in the end.

Was it worth dying for?

Was it worth her killing for?

She bent down and checked her foot. From what she could see the blood flow was minimal. She still had a hard time standing on it. She stood, then closed her eyes when a pair of hands ran themselves around her shoulders from behind.

"Ready?" Tony Sterpanko said.

"Almost," she replied. A tear leaked from the corner of her eye.

"Do you want to be left alone?"

Anna opened her eyes and settled them on the water flowing toward the drain. It was already beginning to run clear. It was also beginning to be difficult to see with all the steam. "No. Not anymore." *Good bye, Mick.*

She turned and stepped through the cage door with Sterpanko. He didn't seem to notice her limping.

As he walked with her with his arm tight around her waist she didn't know what she'd do now that Mick was gone. Her sacrifice in teaming with Sterpanko was meant to save Mick's life not end it. Even with how she treated Mick, she thought it'd be enough to show Sterpanko she was on his side and he'd let Mick go. Only the first part came true. If only he hadn't fought.

Anna stumbled and knelt down and massaged her foot near the wound. Her skin was still moist from getting sprayed. The burn was bright red. A little more blood oozed out.

"What happened?" Sterpanko asked.

"Nothing. Just a little accident."

"You okay?"

"I think so." She re-examined the wound again.

She stood up, took Sterpanko's arm and moved a couple of steps. Heat filled her foot and she collapsed, screaming.

"Anna! What's wrong?" Sterpanko asked, immediately down by her side.

"I don't know. I don't—my foot. The water. I—" Man, did it hurt.

Her heart beat faster and faster, thundering in her chest in wild panic. Then, almost as quickly as it sped up, it calmed down.

She moved to wipe the blood forming over her eyes but no matter what she did, she couldn't wipe the redness away.

Calm inside. Utter calm.

Then nothing.

She was neither hot nor cold.

Just pissed off . . . and hungry.

BONUS BATTLE

MICK'S FIRST FIGHT
NINJA VS ZOMBIE
BET: $30

THIS WASN'T HOW it was supposed to work, Mick Chelsey knew. In the old days, you went out, got a job and gave it your best in the hopes of getting a raise so you could provide a better life for your family.

Nowadays, it was more about just getting back on your feet after the economic system collapsed during the Zombie War. During those dark times, money faded, currencies lost their value, and any that did survive were restructured into a new financial system. The computers had gone down and the backup data was destroyed in one bomb-ignited inferno after another. Everybody was at square one.

Except the elite, of course. Somehow, they managed to hang onto their fortunes and if any portion was lost, the amount was manageable compared to what remained.

Mick, unfortunately, lost everything. The only money he had left over was the little he and his wife, Anna, had kept on their person during the Zombie War—all four hundred-eighty-three dollars of it—and the fifty dollars he now had in his pocket.

They had a house, one of the few left standing after the Zombie War. It was in rough shape, but it did the trick. Since a lot of the records of who owned what had perished during the war—as did most of those who owned property—remaining houses were up for grabs. Humanity had taken on an all-for-one attitude during the war, but the moment the undead were captured and victory was declared, it was back to the old ways of every man for himself. The big houses left standing were the first to be occupied, then slowly the average-sized abodes then, finally, the small stuff. After that, the small stuff in the old bad parts of town. That's where Mick got his house, he and Anna's journey back into the city taking more than a week. By the time they got back, pretty much everything was taken.

Mick double checked the bills in his pocket. Fifty bucks.

Anna deserves better than what she's getting, he thought. She was a princess, pure and simple. Princesses deserved castles and right now the poor girl was living like a pauper. Mick wouldn't have it; especially after all they'd gone through. The bloodshed, the terror, the running, the pain—they needed their life back and not just that, but a *normal* life, one where you didn't have to worry about where your next meal came from or reaching into your pocket and pulling nothing out other than lint.

Blood Bay Arena's parking lot was full tonight. Mick had heard a couple guys talking outside Stevie's Pub that they'd made a nice chunk of change here, something to the tune of seven hundred bucks. Boy, he could use that kind of money. He wondered if he could turn this fifty he had into something more.

Anna wasn't expecting him home for a while. Going in and placing a bet might be a good way to pass the time.

Mick slowly strolled over to the building, hoping he was making the right decision. When he entered the front doors he walked up a short flight of stairs then noticed a couple of burly security guards taking tickets. He glanced around the foyer and spotted the ticket counter on the left. He went over. The chubby lady with short black hair behind it spoke in between smacks of her gum.

"Welcome to Blood Bay Arena," she said. "Here for the show?"

Mick cleared his throat. "Um, yeah."

"How close you want it?"

"Um . . . to the fight?"

"Yes, sir."

"You know, whatever's cheapest. I really don't care."

"Okay." She tapped her touch screen. "Twenty dollars even and you're in."

"Twenty?"

"Twenty."

He fished out his wallet from his pocket and pulled out a wrinkly twenty-dollar bill. He slid it through the small opening at the bottom of the Plexiglas window. She grabbed it, checked its authenticity under a black light, then stuck it in the till and punched a few numbers on her register. A ticket spat out of a small slit in the brushed nickel countertop in front of her. She passed it to him.

"Enjoy the show," she said.

"Yeah." He wondered if he should inquire here about betting or just wait until he was past the guards. "Thanks."

He went back in the direction he came, gave the guard his ticket and was let through no problem.

The next set of doors was set up almost like a toll booth except instead of passing cars, it was passing people. Mick waited in line and about five minutes later was speaking to a skinny bald man with a headset and a nametag that read NICKY.

"I.D., please," Nicky said.

Mick pulled out his wallet again and sifted out his I.D. card. He gave it to the man.

Nicky swiped it in a slot beside his computer monitor. "Pot?"

"Excuse me?"

"Pot."

"Pot? I thought—"

"How much are you putting in your pot? You know, the thing you draw from when betting on the fights?"

"Oh. Um, here." He handed the man the remaining thirty dollars.

The man took it, punched a few numbers on his touch screen, then re-swiped Mick's I.D. He handed the card back to him.

"Look, obviously you're new here," Nicky said. He pointed to the door just outside his booth. "You'll hear a buzzer. Go through there, find your seat, then take a Controller out of the seat in front of you."

"A Controller?"

"Yeah, a little black box thing. You won't miss it. It's a small computer. It'll tell you about who's fighting. Slide your I.D. through the machine, pick your winner, and then wait for the fight to start. If you win, you come back here on the way out and we'll swipe your card. You'll get your money and you'll go. If you lose and end up owing the House, then you'll pay up. Got it, cowboy?"

Mick nodded. *Take a Controller and make a bet. Oh, and swipe my card in it, too.* "Sure. Um, thanks."

Nicky nodded. "Go to the door. I'll let you in."

Mick did. A low drone sounded. He opened the door and entered.

Once inside the hallway beyond, he checked his ticket for his seat assignment and made his way there.

It was pretty far back, the nosebleeds. He didn't care. It was the cheapest ticket.

"Twenty bucks for this?" he said and sat down. "Let's

just get screwed even more." *Story of my life.*

Below, past the sea of heads, there was a giant circle-shaped cage that looked to have a radius of some thirty feet. Its floor was cement. The walls and ceiling of it were made of what appeared to be a strong chain-link mesh of some kind. On opposite sides of the circle's floor were two large iron rings.

Mick tapped his feet then grabbed the Controller out of the seat in front of him.

"Okay, let's see here," he said. The moment his finger tapped the screen, it flashed on.

Swipe I.D. card, it read.

Mick got out his I.D. and swiped it along the side of the machine.

Thank you.

Processing . . .

Welcome to Zombie Fight Night, Mick Chelsey. Please review the information for the first bout.

Mick tapped the appropriate button on the screen and was treated to the details of the next fight. "Interesting. Who else is up tonight?" But he couldn't find a next button or anything indicating such. *Can only see the info of one fight at a time?* "Hm." He shrugged his shoulders.

Staring at the two fighters he wondered who he should pick. He'd seen both people and zombies prevail over each other during the Zombie War. Hard to say who'd win on this one.

"Well, let's go with this guy," he said. He was then prompted to place his bet. He had only thirty bucks in the pot and not a whole heck of a lot of time to waste here at Blood Bay Arena so he decided to lay it all down. Not only did he pick a winner, but he guessed the length of the bout and who of the two would be pulverized over the other. Ten-to-one shot at winning, but he figured it'd be a nice payout if he nailed it.

Thank you. Enjoy the fight, the screen said.

Mick put the Controller back, folded his hands and waited.

Not long after, the lights went out.

Being one with the dark wasn't anything new for Kanaye. If anything, the past fifteen years were nothing but living in the dark, half the time physically, the other half mentally.

No one knew he was a ninja, not even his family. Though ninja's weren't heroes, he took up the mantle of one during the Zombie War, sticking to the shadows, tracking his mother's and sister's movements each day for ten long years as they moved from place to place, trying to stay alive and ward off the undead. There was a price, though. His mother and sister thought he was dead. Before the war, when he first donned his black *shinobi shōzoku* and covered his face with a *tenugui,* he never told them. Even before then he never told them about the long hours after school and university studying ninjutsu, mastering the art. Even the school he studied at was a secret. It didn't even have a name, but instead was led in an old abandoned warehouse on a Tokyo pier by Master Xu—a seventh generation ninja—four nights a week.

He knew his mother would never understand fighting nor would his sister. Both were conservative women and despite their strong sense of tradition, they abhorred violence for it was brutality that took Kanaye's father away from them when Kanaye was just eight years old. His father had been the target of a ninja assassin. The murderer was never found, but the theory was his father bore a remarkable resemblance to a criminal leader at the time and was mistakenly killed as a result.

Kanaye took up ninjutsu as a means of vengeance, unaware in those early days there was more than one ninja clan in Japan. He thought that by joining he'd work his way up the ranks and discover who his father's killer had been. It never came to pass.

The darkness. It was where he kept himself in daylight hours, the real Kanaye secluded deep within his mind, the ninja inside clinging to the shadows of his heart while on the outside emitting the façade of a student fascinated with computer science.

He wasn't home when the Zombie War began and his mother and sister had escaped the house while he was at school. That same night he was to go on a field exercise for Master Xu, but instead of doing so he donned his *shinobi shōzoku* and set out to find his family.

He rescued them as a pack of zombies tried to corner them near Satō Noodles.

After the war, he didn't know if he could face his family and tell them he was still alive. They already grieved for him and appeared to be moving on. Besides, he still hadn't found his father's killer. When Zombie Fight Night started, he thought maybe there his father's assassin would surface if the fiend was still alive, so he made his way into the fighting circuit, hoping that eventually he and the assassin would cross paths.

Now, the darkness surrounding Kanaye was like a warm blanket, a sense of comfort. He dreaded the moment when the lights would burst on, not for their brightness but for what they represented: life away from the shadows. He had been secreting himself in the night for so long that living in the light like most others . . . .

He didn't know if he could do it or even remember how.

The buzzer sounded and the arena lit up.

Kanaye let his eyes adjust as the iron ring across from him filled with blue light.

It slid to the side and the dead began to rise.

The zombie came to the surface, filthy baggy clothes and all. The tarnished shackles around its wrists matched the leathery blotches marking its gray skin. Its facial hair was patchy and wiry. It wore a bandana, one that was red and ripped on the left side, a puff of crusty and dry black hair poking out. The sash around the creature's waist was especially interesting and bore a gold embroidered flower against a satiny-smooth brown that was clean and out of place against the filthy ghoul. The stench of rot and years of decay caused Kanaye's stomach to twitch despite his years of training to withstand unpleasant smells and bad foods.

Pirates, Kanaye thought. The one before him must have come from another time because he hadn't heard of the pirates of today still wearing their clothes of old, yet he also didn't discount the possibility. The oceans and seas were vast and there were still many islands and secret inlets yet to be discovered. Some crews could have held up in those covert places for generations enjoying their previous spoils.

The buzzer sounded again and the pirate's shackles clanged to the floor.

The man shuffled toward Kanaye, arms outstretched. This was going to be easy. Analyzing his opponent was ingrained within him and each of the zombie's movements—obvious or subtle—registered inside a couple of seconds. Slow shuffle of feet. Hands shaky thanks to the rotting arms with barely the strength to hold themselves up. Mouth open, ready to bite down hard. One eye gouged to pieces; the other missing an eyelid. Options to counter: plenty.

Unlike the other fighters Kanaye knew of, he wasn't obligated to give the audience a show. If anything, the only preference Tony Sterpanko gave him was to "do that spinning stuff you guys do and jump around a lot," and even then, those items weren't mandatory.

Kanaye let the zombie get close and just when the dead pirate moved to grab him, Kanaye ducked and slid to the left, executing a sharp side kick into the zombie's ribs. The pirate folded to the right, his body now nearly in half. He stumbled a few steps away. If Kanaye hadn't withheld his strength, he could have easily sent his foot through the zombie's flesh.

The dead man growled. Kanaye covered ground quickly, crossing one foot in front of the other. He jumped in the air, spun and snapped his foot out, the side of his foot spiking the zombie in the nose. The creature's head jerked back from the impact.

The crowd cheered.

Kanaye stepped in, not allowing the zombie to recover, and delivered two swift punches to the creature's chest, a fast right hook to its face, then a spinning back hand hard against its jaw. The ghoul teetered to the side, confusion written on its face.

Practice dummy, Kanaye thought. Upon studying these creatures, they didn't seem to feel pain but instead only impacts and jolts, anything that upset their stride.

Kanaye decided to pour on the assault, but not before drawing some blood. He viewed this particular fight as training. The pirate moved in. Kanaye let it grab his arm. He then took its wrist in one hand and slammed the palm of the other against the creature's elbow, popping the bone through the flesh. Creamy black blood splashed out.

With a swift heel, he stomped on the zombie's knee, his foot cleaving the knee cap off. Blood stained the creature's pants. He kicked the same spot again, folding the knee against the joint. The dead man's leg went inward then snapped off completely. Kanaye avoided a quick nip to his hand and socked the creature in the face, derailing its searching mouth for a moment, then grabbed the thing by the collar, dragged it around and punched it straight in the chest. The zombie's severed leg fell out of its pants as the creature flew back against the cage.

A look of almost disbelief and anger flashed across its face, as if saying all it wanted was a meal and Kanaye denied him that.

You better believe I did, Kanaye thought.

The dead man pushed off from the cage, teetered on the one leg, then began falling forward.

Kanaye darted in, brought his lead foot around in a sharp crescent kick from inside right to outside left and snapped his heel across the zombie's head so fast that, combined with the dead man falling face first, he swiftly guided the creature to the ground, his foot still against its head.

Sticking his fingers out and hardening his hand like a board, Kanaye shoved his wooden-like fingertips into the back of the zombie's neck, breaking it. Another hit and he punctured the flesh. A quick jerk upward with his other hand holding the zombie's tuft of hair through the bandana and the head was removed from the body. Blood leaked out from the neck.

Kanaye stood, dropped the head, then waited for the lights to go out so he could vanish once more.

I won! Mick thought. *I won! Man, three hundred bucks just like that. In the old days that took me two days to earn, a whole sixteen hours. Three hundred beans. Clams. Moola.*

Anna was going to be thrilled, he knew, and, boy, did they need the cash. Now they could get a fresh batch of groceries, get some much-needed clothing and not feel the pinch for once.

"She's gonna love me for this," he said softly.

He leaned forward and picked up the Controller and scrolled to the next fight. He liked what he saw.

Okay, quick debate: I could go and give Anna the money. She'll kiss me and we might even make love tonight. It's been a long time since we did that, her mood kind of deterring things in that arena. Anna. Her perfect—okay, focus. Go, or stay here and see what happens. Maybe just a small bet, like, ten bucks? I could double that. Three-twenty. 'Kay, fifty bucks. If I win, I'm up to four hundred. Oh man. Yeah. Four hundred. His heart rate picked up at the thought. *Three hundred. Wow, but double or nothing could mean six hundred beans before the night's out. That's groceries, clothes, maybe a new front door 'cause the one we have now has a huge crack in it.* And doors weren't cheap. *Six hundred. Six hundred. Six hundred . . .*

He let out a slow exhale through pursed lips. Quietly to himself: "Six hundred, if I win." He squeezed the Controller tight. "Just do it." His fingers wouldn't move. *I should go.* But his legs wouldn't budge either. *Six hundred, maybe more if I put a guess on someone just obliterating the other guy.* "Six hundred." He exhaled slowly again. "Okay, just get it out. Just do it." He worked his fingers quickly, laying it all down on the line.

Man, I'm stupid. Dumb move. He checked the screen to see if there was an option to cancel his bet. There wasn't. *No turning back now. Anna's gonna kill me if I blow it. But I also don't have to tell her. Just say I lost the fifty bucks I started with and it's all good. She can live with that. I hope.*

He put the Controller back and tried to ignore the sweat forming all over his body.

Thee hundred bucks on the line.

Double or nothing.

What could go wrong?

ABOUT THE AUTHOR

A.P. Fuchs is the author of many novels and short stories, most of which have been published. He is also known for his superhero series, *The Axiom-man Saga*, and is the author of *Blood of the Dead*, the first novel in the shoot 'em up zombie trilogy, *Undead World*. He also edited the zombie anthologies *Dead Science* and *Vicious Verses and Reanimated Rhymes: Zany Zombie Poetry for the Undead Head*.

Fuchs lives and writes in Winnipeg, Manitoba, with his wife, Roxanne, and two sons, Gabriel and Lewis.

Visit his corner of the Web at
www.canisterx.com

Check out the *Undead World Trilogy* at
www.undeadworldtrilogy.com

A.P. Fuchs
Zombie Collection

Axiom-man
The Dead Land
ISBN 978-1-897217-83-2

Blood of the Dead
ISBN 978-1-897217-80-1

Dead Science
ISBN 978-1-897217-85-6

Vicious Verses and
Reanimated Rhymes
ISBN 978-1-897217-95-5

Available at Amazon.com, BarnesandNoble.com
or your favorite online retailer.

Also available through your favorite bookstore.

COSCOM ENTERTAINMENT

Where Imagination is Truth

www.coscomentertainment.com